Ice Dreams

candY APPLe books... JUST FOR you.
sweet. Fresh. FUN. take a bite!

Ice Dreams

By Lisa Papademetriou

SCHOLASTIC INC.

New York   Toronto   London   Auckland
Sydney   Mexico City   New Delhi   Hong Kong

ISBN 978-0-545-21126-0

12 11 10 9 8 7 6 5 4 3 2 1   11 12 13 14 15 16/0

Printed in the U.S.A.   40
First printing, January 2011

For Natalie Kaye

Chapter One

Rosa!

Miss u already! Tell ur mom to get you a cell so we can txt. Sammie sez lunch isn't the same without those yum cookies ur mom makes. xo, Jessica

"What about this one?" My little sister, Amelia, held up a photograph of a woman with short hair, puffed into spikes.

"She looks like an exotic cactus," I told her.

"Rosa! That's the *point*!" Amelia huffed and kicked her legs against her chair. Her toes barely scraped the salon's pale wood floor. "I want to make a *statement*!"

"A statement like, 'I'm wearing a colorful blowfish on my head'?" I asked her. "Is that really how you want to start school here?"

Amelia huffed again. Grumbling, she turned the page. "Ooooh!" Her eyes lit up.

Our mother appeared and frowned down at the photo Amelia was admiring. Blond hair with pink tips. "Not appropriate for fourth grade," Mom announced.

With a dramatic sigh, Amelia shut the hairstyle book and placed it back on the table, along with the other portfolios.

"You have gorgeous hair, Amelia," Mom told her. "You don't need a crazy cut or wild color."

"I'm sick of my hair!" Amelia wailed dramatically. She tossed her long, jet-black locks over her shoulder and pretended to fuss with them, as if they'd been causing a ruckus on her head.

"Fine, you can tell it to the stylist," Mom said.

"Ms. Hernandez?" The receptionist, Renee, smiled at my mother. She was a pretty woman with gray eyes and short platinum hair, and she gestured over her shoulder. "Angela is ready."

2

"Rosa, you're next," Mom told me as she took Amelia by the hand.

"Is there anything I can get you while you wait?" Renee asked me. "We have juice, tea, seltzer water, and hot cocoa."

"I'm fine, thanks," I told her. "I've got my glass of water."

"Just let me know if you need anything," Renee said before retreating to her desk.

I sat back in the plush leather chair and flipped through a celebrity magazine. Sometimes, the way people treated me in my mom's salons made me a little uncomfortable. It was bad enough when we lived in Miami, and she was southeast regional director for the Athena brand. But now they'd made her executive vice president and moved us to Chicago. When Amelia and I showed up for our haircuts, Mom let it drop that she was a bigwig from corporate. Now everyone was falling all over themselves for our sake. But I didn't need cocoa and a chair massage — all I wanted was a trim. I had to start at a new school the next day, and I didn't want to look raggedy.

I flipped another page, checking out the reviews of a couple of new movies, when I heard someone say, "Ex-cuse me? Are you *kidding*?"

I looked up and saw Renee blushing madly. "I'm sorry. There's been a mix-up, and someone is scheduled against your appointment."

A girl with gorgeous strawberry blond curls was standing in front of the reception desk, her arms folded across her chest. She looked like she was about my age. A petite woman with light brown hair placed a hand on the girl's shoulder. "Look, we made an appointment for my daughter, and we expect you to honor it." Her voice had an edge. I'd seen her type before — she would pitch a fit if she didn't get what she wanted.

"What's the name again?" Renee asked.

"Jacqueline Darcy," the girl said.

Renee shook her head as she flipped through the calendar. "I don't see your name . . ."

"Isn't another stylist available?" her mother demanded.

"I'm sorry, but we're all booked —"

"Is there a problem here?" my mother asked as she strode up to reception. She had on dark jeans and a T-shirt with a bright red cardigan, but somehow managed to look Very Official. Maybe it's the way she walks. "How can I help you?"

"There was a mistake in the booking, and this girl's appointment got bumped," Renee explained to my mother. She looked like she wished someone would dig a hole for her to hide in. I felt so bad for her, I would've grabbed a shovel, if I had one.

But Mom didn't go ballistic. She just nodded. "Well, luckily, that problem is easily fixed. She can take Rosa's appointment." Mom looked over at me, her head slightly cocked. It was an expression I knew well. It meant, "You will back me up on this, or there will be extreme consequences for you later."

I looked at the girl. Honestly, her hair looked great — she didn't even need a haircut. Still, I knew my mother's motto: "Even when the customer is wrong, they're right." I just sighed. "No problem."

Jacqueline smiled gratefully at me. "Thank you *so* much! I've got this really important presentation tomorrow, and I want to look decent."

Very important presentation? I wondered what that could possibly be, but decided not to ask. "Okay, well, good luck with that," I told her.

Renee stood up. "Well, if you'd just follow me, Jacqueline . . ."

"Everyone calls me Jacqui."

"I'll be back in an hour," Jacqui's mother said, giving her daughter a quick peck on the cheek.

"Thanks again!" Jacqui called as she followed Renee to the sinks.

I waved. Mom came over and pulled my long hair over my shoulder. "I'll give you a trim when we get home," she promised.

I gave her a dubious look. "You haven't cut hair in ten years."

Mom smiled. "Yeah, but I cut it for ten before that. I've still got the skills."

"It's not as glamorous as an Athena spa," I told her.

"I'll give you a few free shampoo samples," she joked. Our house is *packed* with Athena products, of course. Mom gets this crazy discount.

Renee bustled back. "Ms. Hernandez, I swear to you, that has never happened before —"

Mom nodded. "And we don't want it to happen again."

Renee straightened up, nodding seriously. "Never."

"Happy customers are repeat customers," Mom told her.

"Absolutely."

Mom gave Renee a pat on the shoulder. "Great."

Renee stepped back behind her desk. She looked like someone who had just avoided a prison sentence. I didn't blame her for being nervous — I know my mom has a reputation as a tough boss. She kind of has that reputation as a mom, too.

"Omigosh, what do you guys think?" Amelia appeared, flipping her hair dramatically from side to side, like a model in a shampoo commercial.

"Did you get it cut yet?" I asked her. Seriously, I couldn't see a difference.

"Are you *kidding*?" Amelia looked shocked. "I got, like, half an inch lopped off!"

"Looks great, honey," Mom said.

"Yeah," I agreed. "Looks great." But I couldn't help smiling to myself a little. My best friend, Jessica, always used to refer to my little sister as a "Wannabe Drama Queen." It was just so Amelia to walk into a salon, threaten to get pink hair, and then get the world's most insignificant trim.

I'd have to remember to write Jessica an e-mail later. That was one thing about living in a new city — it was hard to have zero friends. We'd been in Chicago for a week, and the phone only rang twice. One call was business for Mom. The other was someone who wanted us to switch our long-distance service. Pretty pathetic.

I just hoped I could make a few friends at school. Like, soon.

Even without a fabulous haircut.

"Ooh, cool!" Amelia said as she bounced along on the bridge between the two ice-skating rinks.

"I know, *two* rinks!" I agreed warmly.

"No, I'm talking about the frozen yogurt place," Amelia explained. "Mom, can I get some?"

Mom dug through her purse and pulled out her red wallet. "Sure. Get me some, too. Anything chocolate. Rosa?"

"Vanilla-and-chocolate twist with chocolate sprinkles."

"I'm getting chocolate with chocolate sprinkles," Amelia announced.

We're a family of chocolate fiends — can you tell? Mom handed Amelia a twenty-dollar bill, and she scurried off to get our orders. The ice rinks were at the center of the indoor mall, on the first level. They were surrounded by boutiques and restaurants. People munched and watched the skaters zip by in an endless circle while pop music played over the loudspeakers. There were two levels overhead, and the ceiling was made of glass. It was a different world from the slightly run-down rink where I used to skate in Miami.

Mom and I went down a short flight of stairs to the large rink's main entrance. A friendly woman with big hair and a big smile greeted us from behind a counter. "Hi — welcome to Wilkinson Rinks! Do you need to rent some skates today?"

"Actually, I'm here to find out about skate classes," Mom said.

"For you?" the woman asked.

"For me," I piped up.

"And you are . . . ?"

"I'm Rosa Hernandez."

"I'm Opal Mission." She smiled, revealing perfectly even teeth. "Have you ever skated before, Rosa?" She pulled out a full-color brochure.

"She's won several awards," Mom announced.

"Mo-om." I rolled my eyes. "They were for the county — where we used to live. In Miami. It wasn't some huge achievement."

"Well, Miami's a big city," Ms. Mission said. "There must have been skaters."

9

"Yeah, but — skating isn't huge there," I told her. "At least, not at the place I went to." I eyed the racks of new-looking brown rental skates behind her. I didn't mention that the skates at my old place smelled like wet stink, or that the average age of the skaters was eight. Oh, or that the place had a giant duck mascot that would come out and dance the hokey-pokey every forty-five minutes.

"Don't listen to her," Mom cut in. "Rosa's a very gifted skater. She'll need an advanced class."

"Maybe we should start you out in intermediate," Ms. Mission suggested. She shifted her body against the counter. She was overweight, but in a pretty way that made her soft-looking. She smiled kindly at me. "If you do well, you can move up."

"She needs an *advanced* class," Mom insisted, her dark eyes flashing.

Ms. Mission laughed. "You're a lady who knows what she wants, aren't you?" she asked.

"She sure is," I agreed.

Mom's scowl relaxed into a smile, and she even managed to chuckle at herself.

"Okay, advanced it is," Ms. Mission said. "That class meets at three thirty."

Right after school. I turned to Mom. "How will I get here? You'll be at work, right?"

"Papi will take you."

Papi is my grandfather, who lives with us. Mom had been afraid that he wouldn't want to leave Miami, but he insisted that he wanted to keep the family together. Besides, he and my grandmother, Lita, had lived in Chicago for a while when they were in their twenties. "Lita loved Chicago," Papi had said wistfully. My grandfather was crazy about my grandmother. She died when I was four, though, so I hardly remember her.

"How many days a week?" I asked.

"Every weekday," Ms. Mission said.

Whoa. My old class met three times a week. Ms. Mission must have noticed my surprise, because she said, "The intermediate class meets three times a week."

Mom pulled out her checkbook and started writing. "Rosa will be in the advanced class."

"Great!" Ms. Mission smiled as my mother handed over the check. "We'll see you here tomorrow afternoon."

I nodded. "See you." Just as I turned and started

back up the stairs, I spotted a supercute guy with green eyes bolting down.

"Oh, sorry!" He flashed me a smile as he ducked aside to let me pass.

I wanted to say "No problem!" but all of my blood had rushed to my head and made me dizzy, so it came out more like, "Noprogrh."

Luckily, Super Cutie wasn't really paying attention to me.

"You're late, Anton," Ms. Mission called.

"Sorry, sorry!"

That brilliant smile shot over my head, and I felt my heart start up again.

"Coach Murphy isn't going to be happy," Ms. Mission told him.

Anton groaned. "I *know*." He hitched his bag higher onto his shoulder and dashed toward the seats to pull on his skates.

"The line was *humongous*!" Amelia announced dramatically as she pulled my cup of frozen yogurt out of the small box the store had given her. She broke my line of vision — otherwise I'm not sure I would've been able to tear my eyes away from the Super Cutie in the seats. "And no chocolate sprinkles," Amelia added. "Just rainbow."

"Okay," I said, taking the dish. I spooned up a mouthful, but I barely even tasted it. I shifted so I could watch Anton pull the skates from his bag, then lace them up. *Is it possible to lace up skates gracefully?* Because Anton's movements seemed elegant — as if he were dancing in his seat.

"All right, girls, let's head home," Mom said. "Hopefully Papi has made something for us."

We started toward the parking garage, but at one point, I cast a look over my shoulder. Anton had disappeared into the crowd of skaters. *But Ms. Mission had said that he was late,* I reasoned. *That means he comes here a lot.*

At least, that was what I *hoped* it meant.

Chapter Two

Jessica,

Tomorrow's the first day of school! Wish me luck, because I'm seriously stressing.

Love, R

P.S. Is it fair that I have to deal with TWO first days of school in three months???

"Did you show her the schedule?" The school secretary frowned at me, making his mustache twitch. The nameplate on his desk read MR. STARK, and his pale blue eyes were giving me a dry, disapproving look.

"I showed it to her, but she insisted that I needed to have a copy of something called the drop/add form," I explained. I'd just been turned away from earth science before I even set foot in the classroom. The teacher had stopped me and refused to let me in until I had the "proper paperwork." Which was weird, because it was fourth period, and none of the other teachers — not even my homeroom teacher — had batted an eyelash when I showed them my new schedule.

"The drop/add form is for official office use only." Mr. Stark's voice was clipped. "Ms. Fontayne does not need to see it." Something about the way he said it told me that Mr. Stark and Ms. Fontayne were used to butting heads.

"Um . . . well . . . would you mind writing me a note, or something?" I asked. "Because I don't think she's going to let me in." Ms. Fontayne was petite and very slim, but she had seemed as imposing as a boulder as I stood outside her door. She acted as if she thought I might try to force my way into class and demand to learn about the layers of the earth and plate tectonics.

Mr. Stark shook his head and snatched my schedule from the counter. Then he stomped over to his computer, grumbling something about extra work and ungrateful teachers.

I tapped my fingers on the old wooden counter and looked around the office. The computers and printers were brand-new, but the furniture was old and kind of shabby. The building was enormous, made of yellow brick, with gray paint on the walls inside and air that smelled faintly like pine cleaner. At my old school in Miami, everything was brand-new, and the lockers were painted tropical colors — peach and turquoise. I'd loved how pretty my old school was, but there was something really cool about Booker T. Washington Middle School here in Chicago. I liked that the building was old. I felt like I was in a real city . . . the kind you see on TV. Maybe in a crime drama.

"Oh, Mr. Staaaa-aaark!" A girl with short black hair and huge brown eyes behind chunky rectangular glasses bounced into the office. "Do you notice anything different about me?" She cocked her head and put one hand on her hip while the other fluffed her hair. Then she grinned, revealing a mouthful of silver with hot-pink rubber bands around the edges.

Smiling, Mr. Stark picked up a paper that had just emerged from the printer. "Your smile seems even brighter than usual." He handed the paper to me, but he was still talking to the girl. "When did you get braces?"

"I just came from the orthodontist," the girl said. "That's why I'm here. I need a note, or I'll have to scrape Ms. Fontayne off the ceiling."

Mr. Stark pursed his lips and reached for a pad of paper. "Yes, Ms. Fontayne likes her paperwork. I guess you'll both be needing a hall pass." He pointed to the slip he had given me. "This is a copy of the drop/add form. She should let you into earth science now. If she has any further problems, please just have her see me."

The girl flashed her silvery grin at me. "Oh, do you have Fontayne, too? Great! We can walk together. I'm Meena Mubarak."

"I'm Rosa Hernandez."

"Awesome to meet you! See you, Mr. Stark." She waved at him as we headed out the door. "Are you new?"

"My family just moved to Chicago."

"Where from?"

"Miami."

"Oooh, poor you! Just in time for winter! Okay, the secret to the cold is that you just have to get really warm, fleece-lined boots and a big, puffy coat and don't worry if you look like the Michelin Man because it's better than looking like Rudolph the Red-nosed Reindeer, with a bright red nose and an icicle coming off the end." She pointed to a classroom. "Do you have Feiker for social studies?"

"Yeah — sixth period."

Meena made a groaning noise. "Famously hard. But gives fun projects. Who've you got for math?"

"Mills."

"Lucky! I've got Jackson. Mills is supposed to be an easy A. But Jackson . . ." She made a whip-cracking noise. She bugged out her eyes and shook her head, which made me giggle.

"Chang for English?" When I nodded, she said, "She's nice, but don't miss a homework assignment, or she'll freak out. I've got Spence. Bo-ring. But at least we don't have Petersen. He spits when he talks. It's like, Sprinkler City."

"How do you know so much about the teachers?" I asked.

"Eh, three older brothers," Meena said. "They all went here. And here we are at . . ." She lowered her voice. "Earth science." She opened her eyes and gave a dramatic, "Dun-dun-DUN! Starring, Ms. Font-*pain*. Who, by the way, hasn't given an A in fourteen years."

"What?"

Meena rolled her eyes. "She gave an A-minus three years ago. That's as high as it goes."

"Wow." I felt my Miami grade point average sinking like a stone.

"But she gives a lot of B's, so don't freak." Meena yanked open the door, and everyone turned to stare at us.

Meena grinned, showing off her braces. A couple of kids applauded, and the rest giggled and whispered.

Ms. Fontayne clapped her hands for silence and stood up from behind her desk. "Silence," she snapped. She turned to a girl standing at the front of the class. "Excuse us, Jacqui, for this interruption."

And that was when I noticed that the girl at the front of the class had curly strawberry blond hair.

She was the same girl who'd taken my appointment at Athena the day before. *Is* this *the important presentation?* I wondered. *Science class?* She'd made it sound like she was going to be on TV or something.

I guess she recognized me, too, because she blushed and looked down at her notes.

"Girls, do you have your paperwork?" Ms. Fontayne asked.

"We sure do," Meena said. She took mine and handed everything over to Ms. Fontayne, who frowned at it as if she was disappointed that she didn't have an excuse to send us back to Mr. Stark.

"Fine, take a seat," Ms. Fontayne said. "Jacqui, go ahead and finish your presentation."

That was it. There was no request for me to introduce myself, no "Class, let's make our new student feel welcome," not even a smile. I followed Meena to the back of the room, where she slid into a seat next to a round-faced guy with green eyes. He smiled at her, and offered her a palm. Meena gave him a high five. I took the empty seat beside Meena while Jacqui finished up her presentation about Mars.

When she was finished, Ms. Fontayne asked the class if there were any questions. There weren't.

"Well, I have a question," Ms. Fontayne said. "What can you tell us about Mars's moons?"

Jacqui looked blank. "Moons?"

Ms. Fontayne huffed. "Yes, the moons. Class — does anyone know the name of Mars's moons?"

Jacqui bit her lip, and I could tell she was dying of embarrassment because she couldn't answer. This is my most unfavorite teacher thing — when they ask you some trick question and then get mad when you don't know the answer.

Everyone looked down at their desks. Ms. Fontayne narrowed her eyes. "Honestly, class, I expect you to read the photo captions in the chapter as well as the text I assign. And Jacqui, you really should know —"

I raised my hand.

Ms. Fontayne folded her arms across her chest. "Do you have something to say, Ms. Hernandez?"

"Deimos and Phobos," I said.

I felt Meena look up at me.

Ms. Fontayne's scowl softened . . . but only a little. "Yes. That's correct. Deimos and Phobos are the names of Mars's two moons. Thank you, Ms. Hernandez, for providing that answer."

Jacqui flashed a dark-eyed glare at me and I pressed my lips together, wondering if I'd done the right thing. I'd just wanted Ms. Fontayne to stop yelling at the class. Besides, we'd just finished a unit on the solar system at my old school, and my teacher had tested us all on the planets and their moons. Was it my fault that Ms. Gutierrez was the world's best science teacher?

Jacqui continued to glare at me as Ms. Fontayne thanked her for her presentation. She glared even as she stomped to her seat.

Beside me, I felt Meena shaking with laughter.

I had a bad feeling that I'd just made my first enemy.

The bell rang at the end of science, and everyone started slapping their textbooks closed and chatting. Meena's round-faced friend turned to me. "That. Was. *Awesome*," he said.

"Rosa, meet Reggie." Meena unleashed her silvery grin. "He's not a Jacqui Darcy fan," she added in a low voice.

"She likes to act like she knows everything — it's nice to see she doesn't. We haven't gotten along since she was my project partner and spent more time bossing me around than working." Reggie gave me a lopsided grin, then stood up and slung his gray messenger bag across his chest. "She was a major pain in the earlobe."

I laughed at his weird choice of words. "Well, I didn't mean to make her mad."

"Oh, you kind of can't help that," Meena said. "She gets mad a lot."

"Ms. Hernandez?" Ms. Fontayne beckoned at me from the front of the class. "May I see you for a moment?"

"That's never good news," Reggie muttered.

I picked up my books and stepped to the front of the class by the windows, where Ms. Fontayne had her desk. There was nothing on it except for a single pen. Behind her, on the windowsill, was a collection of cheerful-looking plants. Ms. Fontayne's hair was cropped close to her head, and she wore large, gold hoop earrings. She had on a long, color- ful scarf, a sweater, and a long skirt with tall boots. She was stylish and would have been very pretty if she were smiling. But she wasn't smiling — and she was scary.

"Ms. Hernandez, I wanted to let you know my expectations for this semester." Ms. Fontayne pushed her chair back so that she could study me. "The end-of-semester exam will cover material from the entire semester. No one is exempt from the exam, which means that you are not exempt from learning the material." She opened a file drawer and pulled out a stapled packet. "This is the course syllabus. It includes every homework assignment. I'll expect you to be caught up to the class by November thirtieth."

"But that's only three weeks!"

"The exam is December fifteenth, and you'll need time to review the material."

She handed me the syllabus, and I glanced at it. *Great.* She was the kind of teacher who gave homework every night.

Ms. Fontayne must have read my expression, because she said, "There are a number of assignments, but most of them are small. You can hand in more than one at a time."

I nodded. I had to bite my tongue to keep from saying that none of the other teachers were making me do the homework for the weeks I'd missed. Somehow, I got the feeling that Ms. Fontayne wouldn't rethink her rules. No — she was the kind who would contact all of the other teachers and tell *them* to make me hit the books. "Okay," I said at last . . . even though it wasn't okay. At all.

Meena and Reggie were hovering near the doorway as I stepped into the hall. "I heard that," Meena said as a flood of kids pushed past us, hurrying to classes. "She's so awful!"

"Seriously," Reggie agreed. "Ms. Fontayne's so scary, I heard she went as herself last Halloween."

"You guys, what am I going to do?" I scanned the syllabus again. "I'll never be able to leave the house!"

"Don't worry, we'll help you." Meena put a hand on my shoulder.

"Yeah, we've already done all of this — most of it's easy questions from the textbook," Reggie agreed. "It's just a pain."

We fell into step as we started down the hall. "So, where are you headed now?" Meena asked. "Who've you got?"

I pulled my schedule out of my bag. "McKay. Phys Ed."

"Five A, B, or C?" Reggie asked.

I looked again. "A."

"That means you have lunch first." Meena's dark eyes danced. "You're with us. Tell me you brown-bagged."

I shook my head.

"Then you'll get to sample some of Booker T.'s finest cuisine," Reggie announced.

"Get the vegetarian option," Meena advised. "It's always the best."

"Hi, Meena." A supercute guy with large black eyes smiled at her. He was walking in the opposite direction.

"Oh, hey, Carleton," Meena said. She grinned, and a pink blush swept over her cheeks.

"New braces?" Carleton asked.

Suddenly self-conscious, Meena pulled her lips over her teeth. "Yeah."

"They look . . . nice." Carleton smiled again, then scurried off down the hall.

"Who was that?" I asked.

"Oh — just my friend, Carleton Connors," Meena said. Her voice was ultracasual, like, *Oh, nobody that interesting*. She didn't say anything more, but her face was glowing like a Christmas tree.

I glanced at Reggie, who seemed completely oblivious to the entire interaction. I could tell there was more to this story, but I didn't know Meena well enough to ask.

Yet.

But something told me I'd be hearing Carleton's name again.

"Oh, what a beautiful place for ice-skating!" Papi exclaimed as we took the escalator down to the rink level. He gestured to the skylights. "With the sun pouring in from above, and all of the wonderful shops!" He shook his head. "It's like a winter wonderland!"

I smiled. Only my papi would think that skating in front of a Sbarro is like a winter wonderland. He's like that. With him, everything is either fantastic or horrible. Usually fantastic. That's what I love about him. He's almost always happy, and he's got a face full of wrinkles that all seem to work together to form one giant beaming smile.

"You will skate like a snowflake across the ice." Papi's hands fluttered in front of him. "In this place, you will seem magical!"

That actually made me laugh. "Okay, Papi. How about if I just try not to fall down?"

He pretended not to hear me, and just hummed along with the mall music . . . which I was pretty sure was a Taylor Swift song redone with string instruments.

We spilled off the escalator right in front of the entrance to the rink. I waved to Ms. Mission, who called out, "Hi, Rosa!"

"Hi! This is my grandfather, Antonio Hernandez."

Papi gave Ms. Mission a courtly bow and placed a hand over his heart, as if meeting her had charmed him beyond words. Ms. Mission giggled. It was pretty goofy, but I'm used to it.

"Is it all right if he watches me skate?" I asked.

"Absolutely. Take any seat." Ms. Mission nodded to the purple plastic chairs at the edge of the rink.

Papi sat down in the front row, and I plunked down beside him to yank on my skates. A couple of other girls were lacing up and stretching. I noticed that both of them had on cute skating dresses. So did the girls who were already on the ice. I felt frumpy in my gray sweats. Nobody had told me that there was a dress code.

Suddenly, a green flash streaked across the ice toward us, shouting, "You didn't tell me you were a skater!"

Meena skidded to a stop right in front of the railing and beamed her silvery smile at us. "Rosa, have you met Atlanta and Delia?" She gestured to the two girls sitting near me.

"Hi." Atlanta gave me a shy smile. Her wire-rimmed glasses slipped down to the tip of her nose.

"Hey, Rosa, you're in my math class!" Delia waved happily. "I remember you because I loved your pink boots!"

"Oh — right! You look different in your skating dress," I told her. I introduced everyone to Papi, who greeted them like long-lost relatives.

A woman in a hot-pink fleece and black yoga pants skated up to us. "Okay, everyone, get warmed up, please," she said. "We're about to get started." I followed Atlanta and Delia onto the ice.

I took a quick lap around the rink. With the move and everything, I hadn't been on skates in a few weeks, and my muscles felt a little stiff and creaky. But the ice was smooth, and I felt good gliding across it. Like a bird just released into the air.

Meena caught up to me and nodded toward the woman in the hot-pink fleece, who was watching us from the center of the rink. "Ms. O'Malley's really nice, and an excellent skater," she said as she wobbled backward. "Whoops!" She stumbled, landing right on her butt. "That's my patented move!" She scrambled back onto her skates, laughing. "I'm totally the worst in the class."

"Oh, come on," I told her.

"No, really — I am. But I'm cool with it. I mean, *somebody* has to be the worst in the class, right?" Meena laughed, and did a little twirl. "I can do a lot of things, but — for some reason — I'm really lousy at going backward. Which makes doing most of the jumps pretty impossible. Oh, hey — Reggie's here!" Meena waved frantically, and I looked up at the bridge that ran between the two rinks.

There was Reggie, waving back. I froze. But not because of Reggie. Right behind him was the cutest guy in the universe — the one I'd seen at the rink over the weekend.

I stumbled and had to windmill my arms to keep from falling flat on my face.

"Careful!" Meena caught my arm and pulled me back upright.

"You okay?" Reggie called from the bridge. I gave him a thumbs-up to show that I was fine. Aside from being half dead with humiliation, that is.

But the cute guy didn't even seem to notice my near-splat. He wasn't even looking in my direction. I wasn't sure whether to be relieved or disappointed.

What was his name again? My brain supplied it as if the information had been implanted there — *Anton*. "I . . . I didn't realize there were any guys in the class," I stuttered.

"Oh, this is an all-girls class," Meena replied. "The guys are on the hockey team. They practice on the small rink."

That made sense. Reggie and Anton still had their bags slung over their shoulders and their street shoes on as they hurried toward the entrance to the smaller rink.

Just then, Atlanta skated around us. "Clear the area," she said in her soft voice. "Greatness has arrived."

I was about to tease her for referring to herself as "greatness" when Meena let out a snort and jutted her chin toward the entrance. A girl wearing a deep red skating dress had just stepped onto the ice. Her strawberry blond curls blew backward as she glided out to the center of the rink. "Jacqui's in the class?" I asked.

"Oh, yeah — it's Jacqui's class," Meena said.

Jacqui lifted her leg and went into a scratch spin, spiraling faster and faster until she came to a clean stop. "Pretty," I said.

"She's a good skater," Meena admitted. "Not that she ever lets anyone forget it."

"Okay, everyone!" Ms. O'Malley clapped her hands. "To the center ice! Let's go!"

"Hi, Rosa." Jacqui gave me a big smile as I skated over. She acted like the rink was her living room, and she was welcoming me to it.

"Hi." *Okay, that's good,* I told myself. *At least she's not mad about earth science. . . .*

"We have a new student," Ms. O'Malley announced. "Everyone, please welcome Rosa. Rosa, why don't you show us a little bit of what you were working on in your last class?"

"Um . . . sure." I hesitated a minute. I didn't really feel like performing a routine in front of all of these people I didn't know. But Meena was smiling at me, so I decided to go ahead.

My teacher in Miami and I had been working on a new short program when I left. I skated to the edge of the ice and stopped, then I took a deep breath. There wasn't any music, except for the mall music, of course. They seemed to have moved on to a piano version of a Michael Jackson dance tune. It wasn't what I was used to, but it would do.

I skated forward and went into my routine. I hadn't done it for a while, and I was surprised at how easily the movements came back to me. The jumps were easy — a double toe loop, a double lutz — and most of the combinations had been familiar even before I worked on the routine. I ended with a hair-splitter and stopped on a dime.

Someone burst into wild applause. Looking up, I saw Papi standing behind the boards, clapping. He let out a loud whistle. I felt my face burning as I skated back to the center ice. Everyone was smiling at me. Well — almost everyone. The smile had disappeared from Jacqui's face.

"That was great!" Meena cried. "Rosa, you should be in the competition!"

"What competition?" I asked.

"Most of the skate clubs in the city are coming here in a few weeks," Ms. O'Malley explained. "Have you ever competed, Rosa?"

I shook my head.

"The competition is only a couple of weeks away," Jacqui said quickly. "Rosa isn't ready."

"Oh, please — if *I'm* going to be in it, Rosa can *definitely* be in it," Meena shot back. "She's *way* better than I am."

"It's kind of true," Delia put in. She winced. "Sorry, Meena."

"Not hurt," Meena told her, waving her hand as if flapping away a bad smell.

I didn't know what to say to that, so I just looked at Ms. O'Malley for help. "Well, think it over," the teacher told me. "It could be fun. This is a non-qualifying competition, so it's open to anyone. Okay, everyone. Let's practice our toe loops. I want as many of you to have a double jump in the contest as possible. Now remember your form. . . ."

I tried to focus as Ms. O'Malley demonstrated the proper jump technique. But it wasn't easy, not with Papi beaming at me from the seats or with Jacqui glowering at me from beneath dark eyelashes.

The competition could be fun? Yeah, right. Like going to the dentist could be fun.

I was pretty sure I was going to skip it. I didn't want to do anything else to get on Jacqui's bad side.

When Papi and I stepped into the house, I followed the delicious smells to the kitchen. Mom was there, still in her elegant black suit and turquoise silk shirt, peering into a slow cooker.

"What are we having?" I asked her.

Mom put the lid back on the pot. "Chicken with corn and chiles. We'll be ready in about forty-five minutes. Would you set the table while I change?"

"Sure," I told her. "Where's Amelia?"

"Upstairs. She's playing with a new friend — Molly."

"Friend?" I repeated. *Great, my little sister already has a friend . . . and I already have an enemy.* I sighed, imagining Jacqui's glares.

"They're making a puppet theater out of our moving boxes," Mom said.

"Does that mean we're going to spend the next three weeks watching puppet shows every evening?" I asked.

"Probably," Mom admitted. She gave me a tired-looking smile, then headed upstairs to put on her usual jeans and navy fleece. I got out the mats and put out napkins, forks, knives, plates, and cups. There were still boxes tucked in corners all over the house, but the kitchen was one room that was completely unpacked.

I pulled my notebook out of my messenger bag and scanned the night's assignments. I had a project coming up in social studies. *Write about a relative (living or dead) who had an interesting career,* Mr. Feiker had written. *Interview anyone you can about the work that he/she did.* I sighed.

"Why the sigh?" Mom asked as she walked back into the kitchen. She yanked open the fridge and pulled out a head of lettuce.

"I'm supposed to write about a relative with an interesting career — it could be anyone. I'm taking suggestions."

"Hmm. Let me think about that."

"Why don't we come from one of those families with famous relatives? Why can't we be related to George Washington?"

Mom tore up a few lettuce leaves and placed them in a colander. "Because George Washington wasn't from Colombia."

"Okay, why can't we have some *other* famous relative?"

Mom shrugged. "Your grandmother *could* have been famous. If she'd tried."

"Lita?" I asked. When I was little, I couldn't pronounce *abuelita* — the Spanish word for grandmother — so I'd always called my grandmother "Lita." "What was she famous for?"

"Well, she wasn't famous." Mom rinsed the lettuce and threw some into a bowl. "But she played a Colombian instrument called the *tiple*. It's like a guitar. She could have had a concert career."

I doodled in the margin of my notebook. "I thought she was a librarian," I said.

"She *was* a librarian." Mom's face looked sour as she frowned over the chicken. "I'm talking about what she *could* have been. She gave up her *tiple* career to raise kids." The way she chopped up a carrot — extra hard, with loads of noise — told me what Mom thought about that decision.

I drew a question mark, then put wings on it. This conversation was not helping. I couldn't write a paper on the career my grandmother *didn't* have. But Mom was in her frantic Getting Dinner On The Table mode, so I decided not to bug her anymore. The project wasn't due for another week, anyway. I'd deal with it later.

I turned to my unending earth science homework. Just then, a herd of wildebeests thundered down the stairs. At least, it sounded like wildebeests. But it was Amelia and a blond, French-braided friend, who stormed into the kitchen.

"Is it spaghetti night?" Amelia demanded.

"Spicy chicken with corn," Mom said.

Molly and Amelia exchanged a look, and Amelia nodded. "Molly's staying for dinner — okay?"

"Sure, honey. Just let me give her mom a call. Molly — what's the number?" Mom pulled the cordless off the wall and punched in the digits that Molly recited.

I couldn't believe it. *Amelia already has a friend who's staying for dinner!* I flipped my book closed.

"Where are you headed?" Mom asked me. Just then, someone picked up at the other end of the line. "Hello, Mrs. Andersen? This is Amelia's mom, Karin Hernandez. Would you hold on just one moment?" Mom placed a hand over the receiver and lifted her eyebrows at me.

"I'm just going to write an e-mail," I told her. "Can I use your computer?"

"Dinner's in fifteen minutes."

"I'll be right back."

Mom nodded and got back to Molly's mom while I trekked upstairs to write to my best friend, Jessica.

Sometimes it's important to remind yourself that you actually *have* friends.

Chapter Three

Hi, Rosa! Sorry I haven't written — so busy! How was the first day of school?

So boring here. Get that cell phone so we can text!

xo, Jessica

"It's kind of a hole-in-the-wall, but they have the best stuff," Meena said as she yanked open the door to Blades and More. To the left was a huge display wall of skates. To the right were racks and racks of skating outfits — everything from short, sparkly dresses to hockey pads.

Meena led the way toward a rack in the back. "This is where all the practice stuff is."

After a couple of days of feeling like a blob in my sweats, I finally asked Meena where I could get a skating dress like everyone else. Very sweetly, she volunteered to show me around the only place in the mall that had "anything decent."

She tore through the rack, *zip, zip, zip.* Meena looks through clothes the same way my mom does — at warp speed.

I picked up a dress with a blue top and a black skirt. I eyed the price tag. Sixty dollars? That was almost all I had to spend — and I'd been hoping to get more than one.

"I know, total rip-off, right?" Meena said, reading my expression. She yanked out a black dress with tiny — almost pinpoint — gold stars on it. "I *love* this! Is it me, or what?" She danced it out in front of herself.

"It's great," I told her honestly.

"I could wear it for the competition," she said. "I need something that doesn't make me look like a pea."

"I like your green dress."

She made a face. "I guess I'm just sick of it."

I looked through the racks a little more and finally decided on a hot-pink dress.

"Oooh! Miami!" Meena said when she saw it.

"Is it too flashy?" I asked.

"Not for somebody from Florida. Which you are."

I started to put it back, but Meena grabbed my arm. "No, seriously," she said. "It's great. You look good in bright colors."

Just as we took our dresses to the counter, the electronic bell over the door bing-bonged and Jacqui walked in. WCG — World's Cutest Guy — was right behind her.

Are they friends? I wondered. *Could this be a date?* My brain was clicking frantically, like a bicycle chain that's come off the guide. *Maybe they just walked in together. Maybe they don't even know each other. . . .*

Jacqui gave us a half wave and headed for the dress racks. But Anton started walking toward us.

"Oooh," Meena said under her breath. "Jacqui's brother is coming over to say *hello*. That's never happened to me before. To what do I owe this honor?"

Brother? I thought just as Anton reached us. I felt light-headed.

"Hi. Rosa, right?" Anton asked.

I nearly fell over. Luckily, Anton didn't seem to need an answer. He just kept talking. "Hey, I saw your routine the other day. You were great."

I was too stunned to reply. Luckily, Meena jumped in. "Isn't Rosa terrific? I think she's got a shot at winning the city title!"

I guess the words "city title" got Jacqui's attention, because she started toward us.

"Yeah," Anton agreed. "You skate with a lot of confidence, Rosa."

"Confidence isn't everything, Anton," Jacqui snapped. "Rosa's going to have to get beyond the basics if she wants to win city." I noticed that she was holding the same dress that Meena had picked up. "She's not going to impress anyone with a lutz."

"There's enough time for Rosa to learn everything she needs," Meena shot back.

I'm never sure what to do when people have a conversation about me while I'm still standing right there. It's always Awkward City. Thank goodness — just then, it was my turn to pay. I passed my dress over the counter. Jacqui headed toward the dressing rooms while Anton looked over the hockey equipment. I counted out the money and took my change, then turned to Meena.

She handed the black dress to the saleswoman. "I've changed my mind," Meena said. "I don't think I want this one, after all."

The woman nodded, and I followed Meena out the door. "Why did you put the dress back?" I asked her. "It was so cute."

"Eh, I really don't need a new one," she said.

I wanted to ask if it was because Jacqui was trying on the same dress, but I didn't want to push her. I didn't want to make it sound like I thought she was just letting Jacqui win.

It didn't seem like that was Meena's style. At least, not when it came to the city competition. And me.

We walked around the mall a little bit. It was late afternoon, and both of us were getting hungry, so we headed over to the frozen yogurt place. Then we checked out a couple of cute stores. "I'm going to have to come back here with my mom," I told Meena. "I've only got, like, two sweaters. And they're both cotton."

"That is not going to cut it." Meena shook her head. "The weather's already starting to turn, and once it gets cold, it won't get warm until May."

"Seriously?"

Meena rolled her huge, dark eyes. "Unfortunately."

I was glad my mom had recently gotten a new promotion. Back in Miami, we were a little tight with money sometimes. But now, Mom seemed to be ready to get us whatever we needed. I still felt weird asking for expensive skating outfits and stuff . . . but a winter coat and some sweaters — that was just necessary.

"Think about all the money you'll save on bathing suits," Meena said, apparently reading my mind.

"You're really making me feel better," I joked.

Meena grinned. "Hey, winter is fun! Especially for someone who likes to skate. Oh, hey! Mind if we stop here for a minute?"

I looked at the window display, which had a couple of large, cardboard action figures in form-fitting outfits. One of them had white hair, gray eyes, and a black cape. Another had long, black claws and fangs. And no, it wasn't Halloween. "I didn't know you were into comics."

"Blame my brothers," Meena said as she led the way into the store. "Did I mention they're nerds?"

Rock music was playing as we stepped into the store. It was bigger than it looked on the outside, and cluttered with posters and displays of action figures, games, and books. And then there were racks and racks of comics. I couldn't help noticing the range of guys in the store — a guy with a giant nose-ring and spiky black hair was standing next to a chubby guy in a flannel shirt. There were older guys and middle schoolers. But Meena and I were the only girls in the store. Not counting the hero-ines on the walls, of course.

"Meena!"

Carleton Connors was waving at us from behind a counter. "I got it!" he cried, then ducked behind the cash register.

Meena's face lit up as she hurried to join him. I couldn't help smiling as I remembered how oh-so-casually Meena had asked, *Mind if we stop here?* Somehow, I suspected that this stop was premeditated.

Carleton's head reappeared. He was holding up a comic, and Meena let out a squeal. "It's the new Grey Shadows!" she cried. "Oh, wait. This is my friend, Rosa. She doesn't know what we're talking about."

"Hey, Rosa." Carleton gave me a megawatt smile. "Meena and I are really into this comic."

"It's not even coming out until next month!" Meena gushed. "Where'd you *get* it?"

"The store got a couple of advance copies." Carleton's face was flushed, and his black eyes shone.

"Can I borrow it?" Meena breathed.

"This one's for you," Carleton told her. "I traded with another guy who worked here."

Meena's face was like Christmas morning. "Are you sure?"

"I knew you'd appreciate it."

"*Appreciate* it?" Meena opened her mouth, but she couldn't seem to come up with the right words to express how much this comic meant to her. I sneaked a peek at the cover. It was done in tones of gray and black, and seemed to be a picture of a person in a cape with a hat pulled over his face. It didn't look all that exciting to me, but Meena seemed like she was about to have a heart attack. "This is the best gift anyone has ever given me."

Carleton blushed. "It's no big deal."

Meena started to open it, then stopped herself. "No — I'm not going to look at it." She squeezed her eyes shut. "I'm going to wait until I get home and I can read it all the way through." She opened one eye. "Would you put it in a bag for me?"

"You won't be disappointed," Carleton promised as he pulled out a bag. He smiled at her, revealing a little dimple on the right side of his face. He was wearing a faded black T-shirt and stylish dark jeans with olive green Converses. *He sure is cute,* I thought. Not as cute as Anton, but superhandsome in an artsy way.

"Can you staple the bag shut so I won't be tempted?" Meena asked him.

Carleton laughed, but he got out a stapler. He put a line of ten staples across the top of the bag. "Now you have to wait."

"Are you *so* psyched for the movie?" Meena asked. "I can't believe it's coming out next week!"

"Yeah . . . the blogs are saying it's great." Carleton shifted from one foot to another. "Maybe we should . . . uh . . . go together."

"Definitely!"

Seriously, I was starting to worry that Meena might just explode with excitement if we stayed there much longer. But the punk-rocker-looking guy walked up to the register with a pile of comics, so Meena just said thank you about a thousand times and then nearly *skipped* out of the store.

Once we were back in the mall, she hugged the bag to her chest. "This is the best day of my life!"

I laughed. "Maybe the best day will be when you have your date," I said.

"Date? Oh — you mean the movie with Carleton? That's not a date." Meena shook her head. "We're just friends."

I lifted my eyebrows at her. "Does he get advance copies of comics for all of his friends?"

"No, but — Carleton and I met at the big comics convention downtown. I was there with my brothers, and he was there with his uncle — the one who owns the store. Anyway, he recognized me from school, and we started talking and . . . you know, we have a lot in common."

I shrugged. "It seems like mutual crush-ville to me."

Meena looked down at her bag. For a moment, her face seemed hopeful, but then she bit her lip and her expression changed. "We're just friends," she repeated. "We both like Grey Shadows, so he talks to me, that's all."

"Hmm," I said.

Meena looked at me. "Carleton is the cutest guy in the whole school," she said. "Half the girls in our grade are crushed out on him." I noticed that she didn't deny having a crush on him herself.

I nodded. "He's cute, that's for sure."

"He couldn't possibly have a crush on me." Meena's voice was low.

"Why not?" I asked.

She looked at me and did her famous eyeball roll. Then she held out the bag and gazed at it. "I just can't wait," she said to herself.

I wondered if she was talking about reading the comic . . . or talking to Carleton about it afterward.

Chapter Four

R: Oh, ugh — silliest thing happened today! Mark D. started a food fight. What a jerk. He's suspended now. Mandy sez they should have suspended Walter, too, since he spilled juice on her. (I think that was an accident tho.) xo, Jess

"Where have you *been*?" Amelia demanded the minute I walked through the door. She was flopped out on our white couch. Xena, our rabbit, was perched on her stomach, like a floppy-eared sphinx.

"I was at the mall with Meena. Didn't Mom tell you?"

"Yes, of course! But I've still been waiting for you *forever*. Molly left half an hour ago and I've been bored!" She put her hand to her forehead theatrically, like a heroine in a cheesy romantic drama from the last century.

"Is that a new bracelet?" I asked, settling at the end of the couch, where Amelia's feet were buried in throw pillows.

Amelia held out her wrist, showing off the sparkly, beaded, pink-and-red bracelet. "Isn't it pretty? Molly and I made them."

"She has one, too?"

"Of course! They're friendship bracelets." Amelia smiled at me. "*Best* friendship bracelets."

I pursed my lips. "Wow — *best* friends? That's . . . great." I didn't add that it seemed awfully fast for best friends. I mean, they hadn't even known each other a week. But I guess that's just Amelia. She's really friendly, and when she likes someone, she adores them. And when she doesn't like them . . . well, watch out.

"Yeah, Molly and Clara — that's Molly's old best friend — are in this big fight." Amelia stroked

Xena's black-and-white ears. "And I think Clara's kind of jealous that Molly has a new best friend."

"Hmm . . ." I wasn't sure what to say to that.

"I feel kind of bad for her. Clara, I mean. She eats lunch by herself now."

"Well . . . maybe you could be friends with her, too," I suggested.

Amelia looked at me with her almond-shaped hazel eyes. "I think she hates my guts. Besides, Molly doesn't want to sit with her."

"I'm sure it'll work out," I tried to sound hopeful. "Clara will make new friends."

"Yeah." Amelia sat up, and Xena hopped off the couch and onto the soft carpet. She padded across the floor and started sniffing at a pillow that had fallen off the couch.

"Where's Mom?"

"She's at work."

"On Saturday?"

Amelia kicked the covers off her feet. "That's what happens when you're the boss, I guess."

"What time is she getting home?"

"I'm not sure — you have to ask Papi. He's in his cave."

The cave is what we call the den. In Miami, it

53

had been basically just a corner of the living room. Here in Chicago, he had his own room, right off the kitchen.

"*Ay, por favor!*" Papi wailed as I walked into the cave. He was stretched out on his favorite recliner — the one piece of furniture he'd insisted that we transport from Miami, even though it was so old and worn that the stuffing was coming out of one of the arms. Mom had begged him to let her buy him a new recliner, but Papi insisted that nothing could be as comfortable as this one. So he was allowed to keep it — but only if it was hidden away in the den. The living room had a pretty cream-colored sofa and matching chairs. It looked like something from a catalog, and Mom wanted to keep it that way. Papi didn't like watching TV in there, anyway. "*Qué fea es esa ropa! Ay, Dios!*" He put a hand to his forehead and his eyes bugged out of his head as he watched a model come down the runway. She was wearing something that seemed to be made out of five or six black Hefty bags.

Papi turned to me. "Who is wearing these clothings?" he asked me. Sometimes, when he's upset, my grandfather's English gets a little . . . confused.

"Why do you watch this show?" I asked, perching on the arm of his recliner. It was enormous — one arm was big enough to be a seat for two people. "It makes you crazy."

"How can I not watch these people and their ugly clothes? They are becoming millionaires by making people look terrible! They call it fashion, and people will buy." He shook his head. Papi watches *American Designer* every week, without fail. He used to be a tailor, and he seems to take the weird fashions personally. "You make that beautiful woman look like a scarecrow!" he shouted at the screen. "And so uncomfortable. How can she sit down? How can she move? What's in the bag?"

The last question was for me. Papi was leaning forward, trying to peer into the navy shopping bag in my hand. "I got a skating dress," I told him, pulling it out.

"Oh, *qué linda*! Now you'll look like the other girls." He felt the fabric, nodding in approval. "This is nice." He flipped over the price tag. *"Dios mío!"*

"I know," I admitted. "Pretty expensive."

"For this quality?" Papi scowled. "This is how things are made these days. Badly sewn, and they charge good money for it."

"I'd wanted to get a couple of them, but I don't want to spend that much money," I admitted.

Papi turned the dress in his hands. "Yes, you need more than one," he said slowly, as if he was thinking. "You skate every day. This will need to go in the wash. You need at least two more."

"But I also need sweaters and boots and a coat and stuff," I said. "I don't think Mom will want to buy everything all at once."

Suddenly, he brightened. "So — I'll make them for you! These little dresses won't take any time at all!"

"Are you sure?" My grandfather didn't really do much sewing since he'd retired three years ago. After making ten zillion wedding dresses, he'd gotten burned out.

"Sure! And they won't look like a trash bag stuck on a tire either," he promised. He picked up the remote and clicked off the television. "Goodbye, ugly clothes," he told the blank TV. Papi smiled at me. "We'll show these girls what a pretty dress looks like, eh?"

"Just something simple, Papi," I told him. "I have to be able to practice in it."

"You don't worry," Papi told me. He put a gentle, worn hand on my shoulder. "I'll make you something nice. Something easy to move in that we can put in the washer without it falling apart, yes?"

I nodded. "Thanks, Papi." I pulled him close in a hug.

Papi patted my head. "Most beautiful girl," he said. "Wonderful, wonderful girl. Just like your grandmother."

It's nice to feel loved.

"When's Mom coming home?" I asked.

Papi checked his watch. "Any minute now. Come, we will get dinner started, yes? Your mother will be tired when she gets home. Whose turn is it?"

"Amelia's," I said. Saturday was our traditional popcorn-and-film night. Amelia and I took turns choosing the movie. I usually pick a comedy, but Amelia almost always goes for a musical.

"Ah, I hope she chooses something with Julie Andrews," Papi said. "I love Julie Andrews." He started humming an off-key version of "The Sound of Music." "Did I ever tell you that I was at the world premiere of the movie *Mary Poppins* in New

York City? It was at Radio City Music Hall. Ms. Andrews was there, and she looked like an angel." Papi's face got dreamy.

"Tell me again," I said as we headed toward the kitchen.

I never got tired of hearing my grandfather's stories. Even the ones I'd heard every week for my entire life.

Chapter Five

Hey, Jessica!

Wait — you're talking to Mandy now? I feel out of it. When I left, you two weren't speaking. Well, I'm glad you made up.

Skating is going really well. I think. At least, I guess I'm getting better. . . .

xo, R

"Rosa!" Meena waved as I hurried to the chairs to pull on my skates. "You look so cute in that dress!"

Atlanta smiled at the hot-pink fabric. "What a great color!"

"Yeah, we won't lose you in an avalanche," Jacqui joked. She was smiling, but it wasn't a very friendly smile. I noticed that she was wearing the black dress covered in tiny gold stars. Her reddish golden hair was loose around her face. I suddenly understood why Meena didn't want to wear the same outfit as Jacqui — she looked gorgeous. She gave me an up-and-down look. "With a pink like that, we can see you for miles."

Delia let out a big belly laugh that practically broke the glass in the ceiling over us. She has the greatest laugh. "That's true, Jacqui," she said. "Maybe Rosa wants to make sure the judges see her, and nobody else." Her blue eyes twinkled mischievously.

Jacqui glowered, smoldering quietly like a coal.

"This is just my practice dress," I said quickly.

"Yeah, you should see the one Rosa's got for the competition," Meena joked. "It's covered in Christmas tree lights!"

"Meena!" I laughed at the whole idea of skating around with a blinking outfit.

"Whatevs." Jacqui bunched up her face in a pinched How Am I Supposed to Deal With These People? expression. "The judges don't like anything too flashy."

"Is that why your last competition outfit was covered in blue feathers?" Atlanta asked. Her face was the picture of innocence, like she was really asking just because she was curious.

Jacqui opened her mouth, then quickly closed it again. She yanked the laces on her skate, tied them, and then stalked out to the ice.

Meena and Atlanta gave each other a little fist-pound, and Delia let out another one of her laughs. "Seriously, you guys," Delia said, "she looked like she was about to get plucked!"

"It didn't stop her from winning, though," Meena pointed out.

Just then, Ms. O'Malley skated up to the railing. "Everyone done gabbing?" she asked. "Mind if we get started now?" When she saw my dress, her expression changed. For a moment, I was worried that I was going to get another lecture on how the judges don't like flashy outfits, but instead Ms. O'Malley smiled. "I'm glad to see you in a practice dress, Rosa."

I nodded. "The sweats were comfier, though," I admitted, wriggling a little. Honestly, the practice dress was pinching me in places where I did not like to be pinched. Out on the ice, Jacqui twirled like a cyclone. She looked so natural in her dress . . . like she went around in star-studded outfits all the time.

"You'll get used to it," Ms. O'Malley told me. "It's important to wear something that isn't baggy — that way, you can really see the movement. Skating is just a form of dance. We're using our bodies to express ourselves. If you can't see the motion, you can't really appreciate the skating."

I'd never really thought about why skaters wore the kinds of outfits they did, but what Ms. O'Malley said made sense. Hockey players wear pads and helmets because they need to. And ice-skaters wear close-fitting clothes because they need to. I guess that's why you never see an Olympic ice dancer in a hockey uniform.

I followed Ms. O'Malley onto the ice. She had Atlanta help Meena with her backward skating. Jacqui, Delia, and another girl named Gabby went to work on spins. Then Ms. O'Malley pulled me aside. "Jacqui and Meena already have short programs," she said, meaning the skating routines for the competition. "I thought that you could use the one you've already got from Miami. We'll just add a couple of jumps. And then I wanted to work on a few things for the free skate."

For the next half hour, Ms. O'Malley led me through the first part of the free skate. It started out slowly, with some lyrical movements, then picked up. There was a stag leap, then I was supposed to skate into an axel jump.

Which is the point at which I fell onto my rear end.

Ms. O'Malley reached out a hand. "Good," she said.

"*Good?* I just fell over!"

"Have you ever done that jump before?" she asked.

"No."

"So — good. You should always be trying to do something that's a little beyond your ability. That's how you get better."

"But . . . won't I make a fool out of myself in the competition?" I asked.

"Not when you master it," Ms. O'Malley replied. "Okay, so here's what happened. You need to keep your rear leg straight. . . ." She positioned my feet and showed me how to take off. Axels are the only jumps that start with a skater going forward. I'm used to toe loops and lutzes — they start out backward. "Then tuck — and release." Ms. O'Malley skated into the jump and performed it perfectly.

"It looks so easy when you do it," I told her.

"That's the trick. To take something hard and make it look easy. So take the next twenty minutes and practice the top of the routine," she said. "I'll be back to watch you and help out with anything you need." Ms. O'Malley skated off toward Meena, and I sighed.

I started at the top of the routine. I really liked the beginning, where I started off with a rocker, then moved into a three-turn and a walley jump. But that's when it started to get hard. A couple of leaps later, and I was moving into a mohawk turn and then the axel . . . and another landing on my rear.

I knew what I was doing wrong. I needed to use my toe pick just a fraction of a second earlier . . . but for some reason, I just couldn't make it happen. I moved through the routine again. And fell again. Grrr. It was really annoying me.

I started again. Stag leap. Mohawk turn . . . and . . . axel! I did it! I stuck it! I looked around, but nobody was watching. Meena, Delia, Atlanta, and Gabby were watching Ms. O'Malley as she demonstrated a doughnut spin. I sighed. Everyone had missed it.

But . . . still. I could do it! Now I just had to do it a hundred more times.

I waited for the music to start again. Then I did the adagio rocker footwork and the three-turn. Walley jump.

Applause?

I glanced up, and just managed to catch an eyeful of hockey players gathered at the railing. I didn't even have time to register whether or not Anton was there. I headed into the mohawk turn and —

Landed on my rear.

I was blushing so hard, I thought my cheeks might melt off. *Please don't let him be there,* I thought, but when I looked up, there he was. Anton was watching me. And when I looked over at the rest of the girls in my class, I saw that they had been watching, too.

Jacqui gave me a little smile. It was the kind

of smile that makes you want to strangle something.

Ms. O'Malley skated over and held out a hand.
"I know you fell," she said, "but that actually looked
better. You just need to take off a little earlier."

"I know." I stifled a groan. "I actually got it —
then I lost it."

"It happens. Keep working — you'll have it by
the end of the week."

"Can't I just fast-forward to that part?" I asked.
She laughed, but I wasn't really joking.

Meena skated over and we both headed toward
the seats. "You're getting that. Let me know if you
need help. For some reason, the axels are easier
for me than the other jumps. Usually."

"Thanks," I said.

"Look who's here!" Meena waved as we slipped
up to the entrance. Reggie was there. And Anton
was right beside him. I think I let out a strangled
little gasp, because Meena gave me a quick Are
You Okay? look.

"Footwork is looking good," Reggie said, and I
clomped onto the floor. It was always hard for me
to get used to regular walking after ninety minutes
of skating.

Anton nodded. "Yeah. But you're going to have to get that axel if you want to win city."

I sat down and yanked at my laces. "I know," I told him. "But I think I'm getting it."

"Rosa's doing great!" Meena said loyally.

"I'm just saying that Jacqui's got two axels in her free skate routine," Anton replied.

Meena was about to say something else, but I cut her off. "Anton's got a point. But I'm working on the jump, don't worry. I'll get it." I smiled, remembering how he had said that I "skated with confidence." *Look confident,* I told myself.

I think I kind of pulled it off, because he smiled back.

"Awesome," he said. His green eyes sparkled, like water in sunlight. He was truly the handsomest person in the universe.

He thinks I'm awesome, I thought. *He just said so.*

Suddenly, I was really glad that I hadn't fast-forwarded to the end of the week. I wouldn't have wanted to miss this moment.

"The project will be on the topic of your choice," Ms. Fontayne said as she wrote *Rocks and Minerals* on the whiteboard at the front of the room. She was wearing tailored black pants and a gray sweater with a loose cowl neck. It would have made me look like a bag lady, but it looked good on her.

Unfortunately, it didn't improve her personality.

"I expect you to work with your partner to come up with a topic by the end of the day," she said. I sneaked a glance in Meena's direction. She gave me a smile and a thumbs-up, but Ms. Fontayne had other plans. She looked down at the notebook in her hand. "Listen carefully. I am not going to repeat this. The partners are — yes, Ms. Darcy?"

Jacqui's hand had shot into the air so quickly that I didn't even see it happen.

"Shouldn't we be allowed to choose our own partners, Ms. Fontayne? I think that we work more effectively when —"

"No," Ms. Fontayne snapped. She shut Jacqui down completely. "Jenna Adamson, your partner is Trace Hawking. Ezra Biggerston, your partner is Mike Messner . . ."

Jenna looked shyly down at her desk while Trace beamed. Jenna was the best student in the class. She'd be a great partner. Ezra and Mike high-fived. *Interesting pair,* I thought. I'd never actually seen either of them talk to each other before. But it looked like they were happy about working together. And it made sense. Ezra was high-energy and creative, while Mike wasn't the smartest — but he was very hardworking.

Ms. Fontayne went on reading names. Most of her pairs worked that way — they seemed kind of unexpected, but like they were so crazy that they just might work.

"Reggie Castel, your partner is Rosa Hernandez."

Reggie looked over at me and smiled. I smiled back, trying to hide my disappointment. I'd really wanted to work with Meena. Then again, Reggie was nice. *I could have done a lot worse,* I told myself.

And then . . .

"Jacqueline Darcy, your partner is Meena Mubarak."

Meena's eyes bugged and she looked like she'd just gotten a whiff of something super-gross. Then she sighed and looked over at Jacqui, who was shaking her head.

Hmm. *That pair is so crazy,* I thought, *it just might . . . be a total disaster.*

On the other hand — someone had to be Jacqui's partner. And it was hard to see who would be easier to work with than Meena.

"Okay, everyone, that's it," Ms. Fontayne announced. "Please take the next few moments before the bell to meet with your partner and discuss your topic and your ideas for the project."

Meena hauled herself out of her chair. "Wish me luck," she said before she trudged over to sit with Jacqui.

"Poor Meena," I said as Reggie slipped into the seat beside mine.

He shrugged. "At least Jacqui's smart. And she works hard."

I lifted my eyebrows at him. "I thought you said she was a know-it-all."

"She *is*!" Reggie admitted. "But I'm not her partner, so I get to look on the bright side." He gave me a goofy grin, and I laughed. "Speaking of Jacqui — it's cool that you're working on that axel for the competition."

"It'll be cool if I get it," I said.

"You'll get it. But even if you don't — it's fun trying, right?"

I was about to say that it *wasn't* fun to fall on my rear. But when I thought about it, I realized that Reggie had a point. Trying *was* fun. And that one time I'd actually made it — that was *amazing.* "Yeah," I said at last. "It's fun."

The room was starting to buzz around us. Ezra let out a little whoop that earned him a glare from Ms. Fontayne. "So," Reggie said once Ezra ducked his head and quieted down, "do you have any ideas for this project?" he asked.

"Not really," I admitted. "I really like crystals, though."

"Maybe we could do something on how crystals are formed," he suggested.

"Oh, perfect!" I told him, writing that down in my notebook.

"The Field Museum has a great exhibit on rocks. We could go there . . . if you want." Reggie blushed a little. I guess he thought I was going to make fun of him for being a Rock Nerd. But as far as I was concerned, he was a total Rock *Star.*

"Sounds great!"

"Great!" Reggie's smile twinkled in a distinctly starlike way. *Wow, he is really into rocks,* I thought.

Just then, the bell rang. I closed my notebook and dropped it into my messenger bag. Meena joined me at the table as I stood up. "Ugh, Jacqui's barely let me talk! She's got the whole project figured out already."

Reggie cocked an eyebrow. "What does she want to do?"

Meena looked over her shoulder. Jacqui had already left the room. "She wants to do a report on famous gems in history." Meena scoffed. "I told her that this was science class, but she doesn't care. She wants the whole thing to be about diamonds."

We headed toward the door. "You should come up with something else," I suggested. "Something you can both agree on."

Meena rolled her eyes. "Good luck. Not everyone gets a cool partner, you guys. You're lucky."

"True," Reggie said, and grinned at me.

"I'll just let her take over," Meena went on. "That's what she wants, right?"

"You should let her," Reggie said. "Because it's going to happen, one way or another."

I disagreed. "It isn't fair that she's forcing her idea on you."

"Eh, life isn't fair," Meena shot back.

Out in the hallway, someone let out a loud giggle. Looking over, I saw Jacqui standing beside Carleton. *What?* I thought. I hadn't even realized that she knew him. But there she was — looking up at him, laughing her head off.

He was blushing . . . and smiling. I sneaked a glance at Meena, who looked like someone had just run up and poked her — hard.

"Hi, Carleton," I said, trying to get his attention. But Jacqui had just let out another hyena laugh. Carleton didn't even hear me.

So he didn't look up as we walked by.

"I think it's pizza for lunch," Reggie said happily. He hadn't even noticed the Carleton thing. "Must be our lucky day."

I looked over at Meena, who was biting her lip. It didn't even seem like she'd heard Reggie.

"Yeah," I said at last. But I knew one thing — it sure didn't look like Meena's lucky day.

Chapter Six

Jessica called. She's coming to Chicago in two weeks. Call her back 2 nite.

    Mom

"Did you see the message from Jessica?" Mom asked as she poked her head into my room. Her black curls were pulled into a messy topknot, and she was in her usual I'm Home From Work navy fleece and jeans. "I left it on your desk."

"Yeah." Actually, it had taken me a few minutes to completely comprehend the note. Like — *Jessica who?* My brain just hadn't been on my best friend at all lately. I was too busy thinking about Meena and all of my science homework and wondering how I was going to master an axel in two weeks.

"So — isn't that great?" Mom leaned against the door frame. "I'm sure you've been missing her."

"Oh — yeah! It's great!" I nodded to show how great it was.

Mom smiled and headed down the hall while I pulled off my skating outfit and changed into jeans and a roomy orange shirt. I was just about to look over the evening's batch of earth science homework when Amelia flounced into my room. "Don't ask how my day was!" she said dramatically. Then she flopped onto my pink-and-purple floor pillows.

Konk.

"Ow!" She sat up, rubbing her head. She'd missed the pillow and flopped onto my floor, which kind of ruined the dramatic effect.

"Are you okay?" I tried hard to look concerned, even though it was challenging not to laugh.

"No! This is the worst day ever!" Amelia picked up one of the floor pillows and tried to throw it. But those pillows are really heavy, so it just fell on her legs. "Grrr! Stupid pillow! Why do you have to be so annoying?"

I flipped my earth science book closed. Clearly, Amelia wasn't going to leave until she told me all about whatever was bothering her, so I might as well ask. "What was so horrible about today?"

Amelia sighed deeply, as if it was going to be difficult to even deal with telling me about her horrible day. "Well, first of all, I didn't eat half of my banana from lunch on Monday. So I stuck it on the top shelf of my locker and I forgot about it — and now it's Fruit Fly City!" Amelia yanked at her glossy hair. "I mean, *gross*! My whole locker smells like old banana!"

"Okay — *yuck*."

"I know! So I had to deal with that. And then, when I got to class, Molly was sitting next to Clara!"

"Oh — so did they make up?"

Amelia shrugged. "I guess. They were whispering when I walked in. And then they *stopped*." She paused dramatically and gave me a meaningful look. "Do you think they were talking about me?"

"Definitely."

"Really?" Amelia looked horrified.

"No." I moved from my desk chair to my bed. "Sorry. I was just messing with you."

"But then why would they stop whispering when I walked into the room?" Amelia asked.

"Maybe they were finished with whatever they were talking about," I suggested.

Amelia gave me a look that suggested that idea was pretty far-fetched. "I don't know. . . ." She touched her nose. "And I can still smell that horrible banana smell! It's like it's stuck in my nose!"

"So what else happened today?" I asked.

"Oh, nothing. The usual." Amelia picked up a magazine that was lying on my floor and started thumbing through it.

"Wait — what? I thought you had the worst day ever!"

"It was!"

"Because your friend was sitting in a new seat and your locker smells like banana?" Honestly, I know my sister is dramatic and everything, but I was expecting a little more.

"And there are *fruit flies*!" Amelia shuddered. "But it isn't like Molly just got a new seat. It's a seat next to her *old best friend*." Her words were heavy with meaning — a meaning that I didn't quite get.

"So?"

"So? So! So — maybe she doesn't like me anymore!"

"That's silly."

"Not to me," Amelia snapped. "And you wouldn't think so either, if it was happening to you."

"Okay, let me ask you something. Was she still wearing the friendship bracelet you guys made?"

Amelia thought for a moment. "Yeah."

I lifted my eyebrows at her, and Amelia's face brightened. "Good point," she admitted. She lay down on my floor pillow and stared up at the ceiling. "Now what am I going to do about that banana?"

"You didn't get rid of it? You just left it in your locker?"

"I don't want to touch it!"

"Get some paper towels and a can of Lysol and take care of it! Jeez! Do you want to have permanent banana smell on all of your books?"

"I took the books *out*," Amelia explained as if it was completely obvious. "I just left the banana in."

"Get rid of the banana," I told her.

Just then, Papi walked into my room. He was holding out something that looked like a dishrag and beaming proudly. "A present for my ice princess!" he sang.

Amelia sat up. "What's that? Where's my present?"

"This is for Rosa," Papi told her. He laid the fabric on my bed, near my feet. "What do you think?"

Now that it was spread out over my quilt, I could see that it was a dress. It was nice, actually — the style was just like my other one. There was only one problem. . . .

"It's great, Papi," I said.

He studied my face. "But," he said.

I blushed. "Well — I'm not sure that brown is my best color."

"It will bring out your eyes!" he proclaimed. "And it will make your hair look lustrous!"

Amelia giggled. "Lustrous!"

"Why is this funny?" Papi asked her.

"Have you been reading the back of the shampoo bottle?" Amelia asked.

Papi looked confused. "You don't like the dress?" he asked.

"No — I do! It's great, Papi. It's just . . . maybe . . . a little . . . plain?" I winced at the word. It had been so nice of him to make the dress, and I really didn't want to hurt his feelings.

"Plain," Papi repeated. He studied the dress.

"It's just . . . most of the other girls have a little sparkle on their dresses. Or color. Even for practice."

Papi thought this over. Finally, he sighed. "Ah, this was always the problem with women's clothes." He shook his head. "I never understood them."

"But you made a bunch of bridal gowns," Amelia said. "Didn't you?"

"Yes, but I always had Lita to help me," Papi said. "Me — I like clothes simple and comfortable. But Lita understood what to add to make them pretty."

"I didn't know Abuelita could sew," I said.

Papi smiled. "She could do everything. Everything."

"Well, maybe you could just add a little sparkle to this," Amelia suggested, picking up the dress. "Maybe a little color at the hem? Like red? That always goes with brown."

Papi looked at me.

"Sounds great," I told him.

Papi gave my sister a kiss on the cheek. "You girls!" he said, then he hurried out the door.

Amelia giggled.

"Are you cheered up now?" I asked her.

She furrowed her brow, thinking. "Yes," she said at last.

"Okay, then. I need to get going on my homework."

"Okay!" Amelia skipped through the door, and I went back to my desk. The minute I sat down, my eye landed on Mom's note about Jessica's message.

I'd forgotten all about her *again*, and now it was too late to call. It was an hour later in Miami. I sighed.

We'd just have to talk tomorrow. If I could manage to remember.

"It's mine." Jacqui fixed her mouth into a prim line. "I was using it first."

Ms. O' Malley turned to me. Her expression was kind of hard to read, but I got the sense that she was feeling the same way I was. *Jacqui has a point,* I thought, *but does she really have to be so annoying about it?*

The problem was that we had each been rehearsing the pieces of our routine to the same

81

practice music. But Ms. O'Malley felt that we should have different music for the competition. It was the only thing that made sense.

"Okay," I said finally.

"I was using that music before Rosa even *got* here," Jacqui went on. "Why should I have to change?"

I didn't bother pointing out that I'd just agreed with her. I think she was just talking to herself, anyway.

I folded my arms. Class was officially over, but we were still standing on the ice near the chairs. Even though we were inside a mall, it could still get chilly when you were out on a frozen surface.

"Look, the competition is only two weeks away," Ms. O'Malley said. "We need to start thinking of a theme for your program."

"Since the music is about autumn, I was thinking I'd do something about falling leaves," Jacqui said. "A lot of the turns and jumps are like leaves on the wind."

Ms. O'Malley nodded. "Sounds great. Rosa, do you have any ideas?"

Yeah, I thought. *Jacqui can do fall — and I'll do the opposite. As in, trying hard* not *to fall on my rear.* But I kept those thoughts inside my head. "I guess I need to pick the music first."

Ms. O'Malley tucked a stray lock of curly red hair behind her ear. "Do you think you can find something by Friday?"

"No problem," I told her, even though I had zero ideas where to start looking. The mall was blasting more of their usual pop-turned-piano music. The scary thing was, it was actually starting to sound good to me. I actually caught myself thinking, *Maybe I'll use this.* But I stopped myself in time. *I'm not that desperate,* I decided.

"Meena!" someone called.

Across the ice, I saw Meena look over in the middle of a camel spin. She spun out, and splayed face-first on the ice. "Oof!"

"Oh — sorry!" Carleton rushed over to the barrier close to where Meena had fallen. "Meena, are you okay?"

She sat up and laughed. "I'm wet and freezing!" she called. "Thanks a lot."

Carleton winced. "Sorry!"

Meena grinned at him and gestured for him to meet her at the chairs. He ran and she skated. At that very moment, Jacqui decided that there was something wrong with the laces on her skates. She started relacing them as Meena slipped into the chair beside mine.

Carleton hurried over. He was carrying something that looked like a small magazine. "Meena, I just downloaded this story from *Grey Matters*," he said.

Meena looked at me. "It's a Grey Shadows fanzine," she translated.

"It's incredible," Carleton said. "You have to read it." He handed it to Meena, but Jacqui snatched it away.

"Oh, Carleton, can you get me a copy, too?" Jacqui asked. "I just love Grey Shadows!"

"You do?" Carleton looked surprised.

"Doesn't everyone?" Jacqui cooed.

Meena looked at me and rolled her eyes as Jacqui skimmed the first page of the story. I could practically read Meena's thoughts — Jacqui had never even heard of Grey Shadows. She just wanted to impress Carleton.

"So, Jacqui, who's your favorite character?" Meena asked.

Jacqui looked like she wanted to strangle Meena. Jacqui glanced down at the page. "Charlie," she said.

"Really?" Meena asked. "Why?"

Jacqui narrowed her eyes. "Um . . . he's just so . . ." She waved her hand.

Carleton looked confused. "Don't you mean *she*?" he asked.

Meena made a little noise that was part cough, part snort, part laugh. She cleared her throat. "Sorry," she said, trying to hide a smile. "I think I need a cough drop."

Carleton reached into his pocket and handed her one.

Meena looked down at the cough drop. She smiled as she unwrapped it, as if Carleton had just handed her a diamond. "This is my favorite kind."

Carleton blushed.

I wanted to die from the cuteness.

Jacqui handed the Grey Shadows 'zine to Meena. "I adore fan fiction," Jacqui said. "I just love people who are really *into* things, you know? Like how I am about skating." Then she flashed Carleton her blinding smile and stepped out onto the ice. She skated forward, gathering speed, then turned and skated backward. The air blew through her reddish blond hair, and she pulled into a perfect camel spin — the same move that Meena had wiped out in just moments ago.

Meena looked mortified.

"Wow, she's a really good skater, isn't she?" Carleton asked.

What could Meena say? "Yeah."

I wished I could just go out there and trip Jacqui. I didn't want her to get hurt — just to fall down. I know that's kind of mean, but I couldn't help it. Meena looked heartbroken.

"Hey, what's up, people?" Reggie asked as he and Anton started down the steps. Hockey practice had just ended. Both of them looked sweaty and grungy — but while Reggie just looked like a guy who needed a shower, Anton looked like he was ready to pose for an ad in a hockey magazine. His mussed hair and dirty jersey just made him look *handsomer*. Like, I didn't even know that was *possible*.

"You're just the two people I was looking for," Reggie said. "Who wants to come disco bowling with me on Saturday? But wait — don't all say yes at once. Have I mentioned that this place has *curly fries*?" Reggie waggled his eyebrows. He looked so goofy that I had to giggle.

"I'm in," Meena said.

"Anton here claims he's a master of disaster at the lanes," Reggie went on. "So it's time for him to take on the Cleaner." He pointed to himself.

Meena snorted. "We call you the 'Cleaner' because you look like you're cleaning out the *gutters*," she said.

"Shh!" Reggie hushed her. "You're ruining my mental advantage! I had him all psyched out!"

Meena looked at me. "Please tell me you can come."

"I'll have to ask my mom, but — sure. Why not?" I wanted to pat myself on the back for sounding so cool, because inside, I was thinking, *Omigoshomigoshomigoshomigosh — I'm spending Saturday night with Anton! With extra exclamation points!!*

"Hey, Carleton, you want to come, too?" Reggie asked, just as Jacqui skated up to join us.

"What are we talking about?" she asked, looking from Carleton to her brother.

"Nothing you care about," Anton told her. "We're going disco bowling on Saturday."

"Oooh, I *love* bowling!" Jacqui gushed.

Anton looked shocked. "Since when?"

Jacqui flashed him a Death Look. Seriously, I was surprised that lasers didn't shoot out of her eyes. "You know how much I love bowling, Anton!" Her voice was all Agree Or Face Consequences.

"Okay." Anton shrugged.

"Um, okay." I could tell that Reggie was pretty surprised at having Jacqui join us. But he wasn't the kind of person who would tell her no way, even though Meena looked like someone had just popped her balloon. "So, let's meet at Strike Zone at six thirty? We can catch dinner there."

"All right — well, sounds like fun! I'm in." Carleton smiled. "Listen, I've got to head back to the store."

"Hey, Carleton," Reggie asked, "do you guys have that video game — the one with the rock monsters?"

"Mountainlord?" Carleton asked. "Yeah."

"Sweet — I'm coming with you."

Reggie and Carleton said good-bye and headed off.

Anton turned to his sister. "Listen, I'm dying of thirst. I'll meet you at the smoothie place, okay? I told Mom I'd be there."

"Okay. Give me ten minutes. I just need to work on my double a couple more times."

Anton swaggered off. The minute the boys were out of earshot, Jacqui turned to us. "Isn't Carleton adorable?" she asked. Then she let out an incredibly annoying giggle and skated away.

Meena watched Jacqui for a moment as she spun into a perfect double toe loop. Then she sighed. "Well, that's it," she said at last.

"What's it?" I asked.

"Jacqui's telling us that she's going for Carleton," Meena explained.

"So what? Carleton likes *you*." Seriously, I had a feeling that Carleton was crushing as hard as Meena was.

"As a friend," Meena said.

"Who knows?"

"We're just *friends*," Meena insisted. "Whatever —
Jacqui can be his girlfriend if she wants. I don't
even care."

That was what she said. But I knew better. She
did care. It was written all over her face.

Chapter Seven

Ro!!!

Looks like I'm coming Saturday! I'm totally free —
let's have a sleepover!!!!!! Yay!!!!!!!

smoochies,

J-Day

Smoochies? I thought as I read the e-mail. *J-Day?
Since when did my friend turn into a pop star?*

*I wonder if she's working on her own clothing
line,* I thought as I scanned the e-mail again. I

paused with my fingers over the keyboard, then started to type.

Hey, Jessica —

I have to ask Mom about the sleepover, but I'm sure it'll be okay. Also, I have this skating competition on Monday, so I'll probably have to practice a little on Sunday. Can you watch me skate Monday?

Love,

Rosa

I reread the e-mail. *I don't have to call her J-Day*, I thought as I clicked SEND. *I mean, I've never called her that. Why start now?*

"Amelia!" Mom called. "Hurry it up, you're going to be late!"

I looked up from the computer in the kitchen. Amelia's bowl was still empty, the box of cereal and carton of milk waiting for her arrival.

Mom took a sip of her coffee and shook her head. "She's usually the first one down," she said, half to herself.

"Tell me about it." I got up from the corner computer table and plopped back into my breakfast seat. I poured myself another glass of juice and took a sip as I listened for my sister's footsteps on the stairs. Mom was right — it was weird for her to be late. Amelia always liked to get downstairs in a hurry so that she could fish the prize out of the cereal box before I got to it.

Mom frowned. "She's going to make *me* late, if she doesn't hurry up."

Papi looked up from the local Spanish-language newspaper. "Do you remember how your mother would wake you up with a song?" he asked my mother, smiling at the memory. "She would sing a beautiful song in Spanish about the morning. It was a song that made you want to face the day. Ah, she was so organized, your mother. And so cheery! She always had you children out the door on time and neatly dressed. All five of you, even when you were running around like naughty puppies!"

I giggled at the thought of my mother acting like a naughty puppy, but Mom just frowned. "Mama was good at running other people's lives," she said. "Maybe she should have gotten one of her own."

Papi looked hurt. He opened his mouth to say something, but just then Amelia clomped into the room. She looked tired as she flopped into her chair.

"No time," Mom said as Amelia reached for the milk. "Sorry, sweets, but it's a breakfast bar for you today." She yanked open a cupboard and pulled out a fruit and nut bar, along with a box of apple juice.

Amelia just shrugged.

"Are you okay?" I asked. Honestly, my sister was looking kind of . . . listless. Her hair looked like she'd combed it with a rake. And she wasn't dressed with her usual sparkle. She just had on a regular old pair of jeans and a lumpy-looking sweater.

Mom tuned in to Amelia's limp appearance, too, and came over to touch her forehead. "Are you sick?"

"Can I stay home from school?" Amelia asked.

"You don't feel warm to me. Do you have a sore throat?"

Amelia looked down at the table. "No."

"Do you feel achey? Do you have chills?"

"No," Amelia admitted.

"Sorry, sweets, but it sounds like you've got a case of the blahs." Mom patted my sister on the shoulder encouragingly. "You've got to go to school. Now hurry."

Amelia sighed, but she took the breakfast bar and juice and headed for the door.

"Hey, where's Molly?" I asked. Amelia and her friend had been walking to the school bus stop together for the past week. I'd just realized that Molly was running late, too.

"I don't think she's coming today," Amelia said. Then she opened the door and walked out.

Papi shot me a look. I could tell that he, too, had noticed that my sister looked small and sad this morning. I wondered if it had anything to do with Molly, and Molly's old-new best friend, Clara.

Mom checked her watch and sighed. "Great. I'm already late."

"I thought you were the boss," I said to her. "Who cares if you're late?"

"*I* care," Mom said. "Besides, I want the people who work for me to be on time. How can I expect them to do their job if I'm not doing mine?" She tapped an elegant fingernail against her coffee mug. "Where's your bag?"

"Right here." I pointed to my messenger bag.

"Got your books? Got your notebooks?"

I peeked in the bag and flipped through my books. "Everything," I said. Before I zipped the bag closed, my eye fell on my social studies book. With a jolt, I remembered that I hadn't done a single drop of work on my project, and it was due at the end of this week.

Note to self: Find a relative with an interesting career. Soon. Or be adopted by a new family.

I hugged Papi good-bye, pecked my mom on the cheek, then swung my messenger bag over my shoulder. Papi stood up to wave at me from the door. *"Adiós, mi amorcita!"* he called. *"Que te vaya bien!"*

I blew my grandfather a kiss, and he pretended to catch it.

I guess I don't want to be adopted by another family. The one I've got is pretty good . . . even if they're a little weird sometimes.

Meena barely looked up from the magazine she was reading when I slipped into the seat beside her on the bus. She was flipping through the pages frantically — like she was cramming for a book report on fashion.

96

"Whatcha got?" I asked her.

Meena held up the cover so I could see. "*Teen Scene*," she said. "No," she mumbled as she flipped a page. "No." Flip! "No, never, no way," she mumbled. Flip! Flip! Flip! "Ugh! Well, maybe . . ." She folded up the bottom corner of the page and then flipped it.

"Are you . . . looking for something?" I prompted.

Meena looked up at me with her huge brown eyes and blinked. "Well, I was thinking I might do something to — you know — switch up my look. Maybe do something with my hair?" She touched her pixie cut. "I like this." She pointed to a page in the magazine.

"That girl's hair comes past her shoulders," I said. "And she's blond."

"Can't I get extensions?" Meena asked.

"You're kidding, right?"

"Grrr! I'm just so sick of my hair!" Meena pushed her glasses up on her nose. "And I'm sick of these glasses! Maybe I'll get contacts."

"Meena, your glasses are totally cute! So's your hair. It's just —" I flapped my hand at her, trying to gesture to her whole look. My friend was actually looking particularly adorable today. She had on a pink sweater and wore a long fuzzy scarf wrapped around her neck. Her short black waves were peeking out from under a purple hat, and she was wearing glasses with purple frames and tiny diamonds at the corner. "You look like *you!*"

Meena heaved in a deep breath. She was still looking down at the magazine, as if she hoped it would come up with some brilliant, life-altering hairdo. "Maybe I just need new shampoo." She looked miserable . . . just as miserable, in fact, as she had the day before, when Jacqui announced that she thought Carleton was adorable. Suddenly — as if a thought had just occurred to her — she perked up. "Or maybe I just need a new shirt or something. Hey — do you want to go shopping with me on Friday afternoon? We could go after practice. Or — hey — we could go Saturday morning. What do you say? Are you free? It'll be fun!"

I studied her eager face. "Does this have anything to do with disco bowling?" I asked. "And the fact that Carleton and Jacqui are going to be there?"

Meena sank down into her seat and put the magazine over her face.

"Meena, you look awesome the way you are. But I'll totally go shopping with you, if you want."

She peeked out from beneath the magazine. "Really?"

"Of course! It'll be fun. Let's go Saturday. I'm always beat after practice on Friday. And if you want a haircut or something, we could head over to my mom's spa. There's one in the mall."

Meena put her head on my shoulder. "Thanks, Rosa. I feel better already."

I put my arm around her and gave her a squeeze. Poor Meena. Jacqui had turned this whole disco bowling thing into total torture. "Just for the record, Meena, you're gorgeous."

Meena snorted and rolled her eyes. But when she looked out the window, I saw her smile. Jacqui's pretty, it's true. But nobody's prettier than Meena when she smiles.

Chapter Eight

Rosa,

What's the weather like in Chicago? How many sweaters do I need? Mandy sez I'll need to wear three sweaters and a heavy coat, even though it's just November. That's not true — is it?

J

"This is awesome," Reggie said when I showed him the research I'd done on crystals. "The pictures are great. Where'd you get these books?"

I laughed loud enough to get a withering look from Ms. Fontayne. She'd given us the last ten minutes of class to work on our projects. I grimaced and lowered my voice. "There's a library two blocks from my house."

"You went to a *real library*?" Reggie looked surprised. "I just looked up some stuff on the Internet."

"I like books," I told him. "The Internet can give you a lot of information, but it can also give you a lot of junk."

Reggie nodded as he looked down at the beautiful photos of crystals. "Tell me about it. So, listen, when do you want to head over to the Field Museum? I was thinking Saturday."

"Sounds great," I said quickly. I was actually really excited to head over to the museum and look at the rocks. Reggie was a great partner — he had a lot of good ideas and made the work fun. I was sure that we were going to have a blast. I pulled out my calendar to write myself a note. *Jessica* was scribbled across Saturday morning. "Oh no!" I said just as the bell rang.

Reggie looked up.

"I can't hang out on Saturday — I have plans." An image of Jessica popped into my head. I somehow doubted that she'd want to tag along to a museum to look at rocks. "Could we maybe hang out Sunday? In the afternoon? That way I can skate for a couple of hours in the morning."

Reggie crossed out the note he'd made on his calendar and rewrote it for Sunday. "Okay, Sunday it is. Why can't you make it Saturday?"

I was about to explain about Jessica when Meena walked up to our table. She'd overheard Reggie's question, and she explained, "Rosa and I are hanging out at the mall on Saturday." I made a little choking/squeaking sound, and Meena lifted an eyebrow. "What?"

"I am sosososo sorry!" I spewed. I grabbed her hand. "I totally forgot that my good friend from Miami is going to be in town that day. I told her we'd hang out."

"Oh." Meena nodded, but she bit her lip a little. I could tell she was disappointed, but she didn't have a freak-out about it. "Okay. It's not a big deal."

I felt like a capital-*J* Jerk as we headed out into the hallway. We were just in time to see Jacqui give

Carleton a playful poke on the shoulder. Meena looked crushed — like something that needed to be swept up off the floor. I wanted to tell her to forget the whole thing — I'd bag on Jessica, and we'd go out and get her an awesome, confidence-boosting outfit. Honestly, at that moment, I really wanted to go hang with Meena. Jessica felt kind of like someone I didn't know anymore.

But Jessica had been my friend since second grade. I couldn't just let go of her.

It just didn't feel right.

Mom hummed along with the guitar music as she roasted the poblanos over the gas flame. The green chilis sent a sweet, spicy smell wafting through the house. My mouth watered as I chopped onions. My eyes were watering, too. And my nose. Basically, I was a big faucet that had just been turned on.

Amelia handed me a tissue.

"Hey, thanks," I said as I dabbed at my eyes, then my nose. "These onions . . ."

Amelia nodded, but she didn't say anything. She was still looking a little listless as she gathered silverware to set the table.

"Are those onions ready, *amorcita*?" Mom asked.

She always calls me her "little love" when she's in a good mood. You'd think that after working hard all day, Mom wouldn't want to cook. I know I wouldn't. But Mom says she finds it relaxing. Of course, she never complains on the days that Papi makes dinner either.

I guess Mom doesn't do a lot of complaining, period. I'd never really thought about that, but it was true.

I handed over the onions, and Mom dropped them into the pan, where they sizzled and snapped.

"Mmm!" Papi grinned as he walked into the kitchen. "Delicious smells are floating all over the house!"

Mom laughed. "We're having beef-and-sweet-potato stew and empanadas."

"Ay, Dios — qué suerte!" Empanadas were my grandfather's absolute favorite. "Ah — you make it just like your mother," Papi said, drawing Mom into a hug. "And that is the best in the world."

Mom smiled. "True," she admitted. "If I do say so myself."

"And why can't we have a smile from you?" Papi asked Amelia. "You're still sad, eh?"

"I don't like school," Amelia told him.

"Don't like school!" My grandfather placed his hands over his heart. *"Qué horror!"*

"Since when?" Mom demanded.

"What's the big deal?" Amelia asked.

"*School* is a big deal," Mom told her. She stirred the pot and added in some tomatoes, which hissed in protest. "What's the problem? Is your teacher giving you a hard time? Is she giving you too much work? I can go talk to her."

I sneaked a glance at Amelia, who was staring at the floor and shaking her head. I guessed that her problems with school didn't have anything to do with teachers or homework, but I didn't know how to stop Mom from going off on her School Is Important rant. "Maybe Amelia just had a rough day. Oh — hey, Mom? Can I go to the Field Museum this Sunday afternoon? It's for a research paper on rocks."

"Sure, I can drop you off on my way to yoga class." In a moment, she was humming and stirring again. Thinking about yoga always perks Mom up. Amelia flashed me a grateful smile.

"Ah, this music — so beautiful!" Papi said as he sat down at the kitchen table. "Girls, your grandmother had a gift."

"Wait — what?" I asked. "This — this is Lita? Playing the guitar?"

"Not the guitar, the *tiple*. This is Colombian music." He shook his head. "Didn't you know this is your grandmother's music?"

I paused a moment, listening to the familiar strains. It was a recording I'd heard all my life.

"I didn't know either," Amelia said.

Papi put his hands to his forehead. "Girls, girls! Yes, your grandmother was a virtuoso!" He closed his eyes and listened. "Ah, such beauty. Music like a flower!"

"Like a flower that blooms in the desert," Mom grouched from her place by the pot.

"What?" Papi looked shocked by my mother's words. "Your grandmother played concerts for others — at the church. She went to the nursing home twice a year to perform!"

"She could have performed at Carnegie Hall," Mom shot back.

Papi looked hurt. "She never wanted to play at Carnegie Hall."

"Who knows what she wanted?" Mom replied.

Silence pulsed through the room. Amelia and I looked at each other. Neither one of us knew what to say. I didn't dare just change the subject again. Finally, my mom looked down into her pot. "I have to let this simmer for a while," she announced. "Dad, keep an eye on it for me, will you? I'm going upstairs to change."

Papi's lips were mashed together, but he managed to nod. Mom turned and walked out of the room. My sister, my grandfather, and I were still for a few moments, just listening, as the music played on.

Finally, Papi ran his long fingers through his hair.

I didn't know what to tell him. "Sorry," was all I came up with.

Papi waved my word away, as if it were useless to him. "Ah, your mother never understood Lita. Karin doesn't understand that not everyone is like her."

"You said it," Amelia agreed.

"For Karin, work is very, very important," Papi said. "But your grandmother played the *tiple* for love."

I sat at the table, glad that I could just be with my sister and grandfather in silence as we took in the music. I felt as if I were hearing it for the first time. The notes leaped and danced, floating like butterflies through the air. I had to admit that I understood what my mom was saying. This music was great — Lita really could have been famous. It seemed hard to believe that she didn't really want to be.

Suddenly, an idea fluttered into my mind. "Papi," I said, "would you mind if I borrowed this recording for a little while?"

My grandfather grinned hugely. "Rosa, it would be my deep honor to give this to you. Your grandmother would be so happy."

I put my arms around him, and Papi pulled me into a big hug.

After dinner, I grabbed my notebook and found Mom in the cave. She was seated in Papi's ugly recliner with her feet tucked up beneath her. She was typing on her laptop, but when I knocked gently on the door, she looked up and smiled.

"Hey, *amorcita*," she said. "What's up?"

"I just wanted to ask you a few questions," I said, hovering in the doorframe. "Are you busy?"

Mom shut her computer and set it carefully on a side table. "Not too busy for you."

I sat down on the couch beside Papi's chair. I took a minute to get comfortable, then fired my first question. "So, what exactly do you do? I mean, what's your job?"

Mom looked surprised, and a tiny smile slipped up the side of her face. "Well, my official title is executive vice president of operations. Basically, I make sure that things are running smoothly in our salons, that people have the supplies they need, stuff like that."

I clicked my pen and scribbled on my pad. "Executive vice president," I repeated. "So, like, if something happens to the president, you're in charge?"

Mom laughed. "Not quite. There are a few vice presidents. But not that many."

I looked down at my list of questions. "What is the biggest challenge of your job?"

Mom leaned back in the chair and thought that one over. "You know, when you were very little and I was still a stylist, I could make my own schedule, so that I could be at home in the afternoon with you. I was still working hard, going to business school at night, but I got to spend time with you. Now, I'm stuck at the office in the afternoons and sometimes on the weekends. And sometimes I miss you and Amelia." Mom's eyes were sad, but her words made me feel warm inside. It was nice to know that she was still thinking about us even when she was at work. "I feel really blessed to have Papi living with us," Mom went on. "Because I know how much he loves you, and I know he takes care of you the way I would."

"We're lucky." I tapped the pen against the pad of paper, thinking about Papi. Sometimes, I actually felt sorry for my cousins, because they didn't get to have him living with them. I couldn't imagine life without him. "So — what do you like about your job?" I asked Mom.

She smiled. "Oh, lots of things. I love making sure that everything is running smoothly. I love making sure that the business runs well, so that we can make sure that people have jobs. I love making sure that people are happy at their jobs. And I like working in an industry where our job is to make people feel good about themselves. You know, I've seen people come into our salons looking tired and run-down. But after a fresh haircut and a chat with the stylist, and maybe a nice cup of tea or something, they look better. And not just because of the haircut. When they take the time to take care of themselves, it shows. They're more relaxed. They're happier. And that makes me happy." Mom watched me scribble for a minute, then asked, "So, why all the questions? Aren't you supposed to be doing homework?"

"This is homework," I explained. "I'm supposed to interview someone who has an interesting career — remember?"

"And you picked me?" Mom looked flattered.

"You have a really interesting career," I told her.

Mom touched a curl that had escaped from the loose bun at the nape of her neck. She smiled a little, and I felt a surge of pride. *My mother is beautiful,* I thought. *And successful. And smart.*

I didn't usually think about her that way — she was just . . . Mom. But it was true. I surprised myself by throwing my arms around her. She hugged back. "Thanks, *amorcita*," she whispered into my hair.

I gathered my pen and notebook and headed

toward the door. Mom was reaching for her computer when I turned back. "Oh!" I said suddenly. "I forgot to ask. Is it okay if Jessica spends the night on Saturday?"

"Jessica?" Mom asked. "Oh, right — I forgot she's coming to town."

"Yeah. We wanted to hang out for a while, then have a sleepover, if it's okay."

"Don't you have your skating contest on Monday?"

I smiled, and decided not to point out that it was a competition, not a contest. "Yeah. I was thinking she could come."

"It's fine with me," Mom said. "I'm sure you two have been missing each other."

"Can I just use the computer to write her?" I asked. "I don't want to call — it's kind of late."

"Ten minutes," Mom said.

I hurried out the door, shutting it carefully behind me. Then I rushed to the kitchen to write Jessica. I was about to start an e-mail when I saw that she was on IM.

myammeegirl: U there?

112

I waited impatiently for her reply message to appear. Finally, it did.

jessme: Hi

My fingers flew across the keyboard.

myammeegirl: My mom said ok to saturday!

It seemed to take forever for Jessica to reply.

jessme: I'm not coming this weekend after all.

I stared at the sentence for a moment. *What? Jessica's not coming?* After a moment, another message popped up.

jessme: Sorry! I forgot the 7th grade dance is this weekend. Can't miss it! U understand, right?

The seventh grade dance? No, I didn't really understand. My fingers froze. I didn't know what to write.

jessme: Listen G2G. Late here. I'll call tomorrow? Smooch!

And — poof! — she disappeared.

I was shutting down the computer when Amelia came waltzing into the kitchen. She hummed a pop tune as she yanked open the fridge. She poured some pomegranate juice into a cup and took a sip. "Ah!" she said with a grin. "That's refreshing!"

I laughed. "Are you on a juice ad?"

Amelia giggled.

"You look happy," I told her.

"Maeve just called me. She said that Molly is having a sleepover party on Saturday!" Amelia smiled. "Maeve said that Molly told her she was going to hand out invitations tomorrow."

"Sounds like fun."

"It will be," Amelia put the pitcher of juice back into the fridge. "Maeve said that Molly is going to show a movie on the big screen she has in her basement, and everyone is going to make popcorn balls."

I sighed, thinking about my suddenly less exciting Saturday. It's pretty sad when you're jealous of your little sister's plans.

"I can't wait!" Amelia said. Then she darted up the back stairs.

It was good to see her smiling again. Maybe if she and Molly and Clara could hang out at the party, they'd all end up friends.

Why not, right?

Chapter Nine

You have no new e-mail.

"Good!" Ms. O'Malley watched, arms folded across her chest, as I moved into my footwork and then pulled a mohawk turn. "Lovely." My new music floated over the speakers, the notes falling as gently as snowflakes. I stuck my pick, then was in the air. "Wonderful!" Ms. O'Malley called as I nailed the landing. I'd done it! A perfect axel!

I spun into a doughnut. "Looking good," Ms. O'Malley called. "Keep that spin tight." Then my favorite — a camel turn. "Nice, Rosa," she called. More footwork, and a single toe loop. This was the part of the routine I loved best. I skated across the ice, trying to fill each corner with my movement. Finally, I came into a tight spin. I pulled my arms up and then — stopped.

"Bravo!" Ms. O'Malley called when I had finished. "That looks wonderful, Rosa!"

I skated over to her, feeling my face flush. That had felt good. *Really* good. Ms. O'Malley was standing with Delia, Atlanta, Jacqui, and Meena. "Rosa, that routine is really coming together," Ms. O'Malley said. "Now, you're going to want to watch your arms on that double toe loop. Keep them in, like this." She curved her arms in toward her body. "That will keep you from getting thrown off balance. And make sure you're giving us as much expression in your opening footwork as you can. Right before the mohawk, you look like you're starting to worry about the axel."

"That's when I *am* starting to worry about the axel," I admitted.

"Well, *don't* worry about it. You've nailed it in practice, so you can nail it in the competition. If you skate as well on Monday as you did today, we'll see you up on the podium." Ms. O'Malley looked so confident. I wished I felt as sure about my routine as she did.

"Your routine looks really good," Atlanta said in her shy voice.

"I noticed that Rosa's arms looked a little sloppy on her opening spin," Jacqui volunteered. She looked like someone who'd just found a worm in her cupcake. "You need to keep them firm, like this." Jacqui demonstrated. "Yours were all —" And she wobbled her arms around, like someone in a major earthquake.

I was pretty sure that my arms hadn't looked that bad, but I just nodded. "Okay, thanks."

Ms. O'Malley looked like she wanted to say something to Jacqui, but she decided against it. Instead, she turned to Meena. "Meena, did you see how Rosa really picked up speed right before the toe loop?"

"Hmm?" Meena snapped to attention. She had been staring off into space, looking out toward the mall.

"Did you notice Rosa's entry into the jump?" Ms. O'Malley repeated. "That's what I want you to do. Speed, then pick down, spin, and land. Got it?"

Meena nodded. "Right. Speed." She fiddled with the end of her long scarf. She had just practiced her routine before mine, and it hadn't looked too good. Meena wasn't the best skater in our class, but at least she usually skated with a lot of energy. Today, she looked limp and sort of spaced out. As if the real Meena was on another planet and had been replaced by a Meena-bot. She'd barely said two words to me all day.

"Yeah, Meena, and I noticed that you completely started off on the wrong foot when you were doing your footwork," Jacqui pointed out. "That's why you got messed up on your turn. If you do that in the competition, you'll fall on your butt."

Meena looked at Jacqui. She didn't say anything, but her eyes filled with sudden tears. Ooh, I *so* wanted to skate over Jacqui's foot.

Ms. O'Malley's delicate nostrils flared. "Jacqui, why don't you focus on your *own* routine?" she snapped.

Jacqui's eyes widened and she looked shaken. "I'm just trying to help," Jacqui said.

"I'm sure we all appreciate your input," Ms. O'Malley said, "but it seems to me that you've got a late jump to worry about."

I know this is mean, but it was all I could do not to say *HA!* when Ms. O'Malley finished. It was true — Jacqui's timing had been a little off on her second jump, and her landing had been slightly wobbly. *Take that, Jacqueline Darcy! How does it feel to get picked on in front of everyone?*

"I suggest you just take the criticism and then do your best," Ms. O'Malley went on. "Like Rosa."

Jacqui turned a shade of red that would have looked lovely on an apple or an iPod. She shot me one of her evil glares, but I just looked away.

Then Ms. O'Malley suggested that everyone pick a couple of elements from their routine to work on for the next twenty minutes. Atlanta chose to work on her spins, and Delia practiced her leaps. It was a little hard to tell what Meena was working on. I think it was her footwork, which was the one thing she had down. Mostly, she just seemed to be skimming around in circles at the far end of the ice. I knew what I needed to do — the same thing I'd needed to do for the past two weeks. Work on the footwork, the mohawk, and the axel.

I skated out to the center ice. I slid out my right leg, then my left. Glide, glide, crossover . . . "Oof!"

Someone slammed into my shoulder and I spun out. My legs slipped from under me and I landed right on my rear end. Looking up, I saw a flower-petal-blue dress skating away at top speed. It was Jacqui. She skidded to a stop and skated back toward me.

"Oh, I'm *so* sorry!" she said. She sounded about as convincing as the fake snow sprayed in the store windows around us. "I didn't even see you there." She held out a hand and helped haul me to my feet. "I guess we need to be more careful." Then she flashed me a smile and skated away.

Meena skated over. "I saw that."

"What was that all about?" I asked.

"That was about Jacqui giving you a warning." Meena looked at me sideways. "She's telling you that she's number one — not you."

Even though it was cold out on the ice, I felt my blood starting to heat up. I watched Jacqui skating over the ice like a hummingbird zooming from flower to flower. As if nothing had happened. *Does she seriously think she can scare me?* I wondered. It was as if Jacqui thought she had a *right* to win this competition. Just like she thought she had a *right* to Carleton. I felt like a piece of paper that had gone up in flames. Grrr.

"Yeah, I'm kind of not excited to go disco bowling with Jacqui," Meena admitted. "She'll probably try to drop a bowling ball on my foot or something."

"If she does, she'll wind up facedown in a lane with a gutterball rolling over her," I snapped.

Meena looked shocked, then started to laugh.

"I'm serious!" I insisted, but Meena just kept giggling. Finally, I realized how silly I sounded. I, Rosa Hernandez, was not about to roll a bowling ball over Jacqui — no matter how much I wanted to. I started giggling, too.

"Okay, maybe this is going to be fun, after all," Meena said. "Too bad you and I can't hang out beforehand. We could think of other ways to handle Jacqui if she gets out of line. Maybe stick a bowling pin in her ear?" Meena giggled again.

Suddenly, I remembered that Jessica wasn't coming tomorrow. That meant that Meena and I *could* hang out at the mall in the afternoon. But just as I opened my mouth to suggest it, Jacqui went whizzing past, and my anger flared up again.

She wants to beat everyone, I thought, my rage exploding. *But she's not going to beat me. Not this time.* Right at that moment, I decided that I was going to spend all afternoon practicing my routine. And Sunday morning, too. By the time Monday came around, it would be perfect.

Perfect.

And Jacqui could just deal with it.

I put a hand on Meena's shoulder. "We'll have fun. It doesn't matter what Jacqui does."

Meena smiled . . . but — like her footwork — it was a little wobbly. "Yeah," she said.

"Believe it," I told her.

"I'll try," she promised.

In my bones. That was where I wanted the axel to be. *In my bones.* I didn't want to think about it. I just wanted to do it automatically, the way your heart keeps beating and your lungs keep on breathing, even in your sleep.

Mom took me to the mall early and dropped me off at the rink, then disappeared to window-shop.

The mall was nearly empty as I skated my routine over and over. The restaurants in the food court were shuttered, each in its own way. The French bakery-café had actual wooden shutters, the Mexican restaurant had locked all of their tables behind glass doors, and the hamburger place was dark behind a roll-down metal gate. Everything was quiet, except for the sound of my grandmother's *tiple*. Ms. Mission was at her place behind the desk when I arrived, and she happily put the music into the stereo system for me. Ms. O'Malley had announced that the rink would be open both early and late in case anyone wanted to practice. But nobody else was there.

Two older women — one black, one white, both with white hair — looped around the mall in sneakers, side by side. They had passed the rink four times in the past two hours. Occasionally, they would pause in their exercise to watch me. Once, they even burst into applause when I nailed my first jump — a toe loop. I smiled, but tried not to let them distract me as I headed into the axel.

Don't think about it, I commanded myself. *Don't think about.*

Too late — I was already thinking about it.

I set my pick too early, and slipped a little on

the landing. I managed to recover, though, and headed into the rest of my routine. That's practice. You're a little late, you're a little early, sometimes you're perfect. Do it five thousand times, and the percentage of perfects goes up.

But you never really hit one hundred percent perfect all the time. I mean, I still sometimes bite my tongue when I'm chewing — and how many times have I had something to eat? You'd think I'd have that one nailed by now.

After a while, I took a break to tighten up my skates. The mall was starting to fill up — the restaurants had pulled back their gates, and a few people were even sitting down, having coffee or breakfast. More walkers were milling around the mall, and workers had started to arrive to unlock the stores.

I sat for a moment, just thinking about skating. It isn't like other sports. It's not like walking, or running either. Some people say that it's like Rollerblading, and that's close. But ice-skating is smoother. There aren't any bumps, no rocks to throw you to the ground.

Once, I had a dream that I could fly. Not very high, only about a couple of feet off the ground.

But in order to do it, I had to run, and then just let myself drop, face-first, toward the pavement.

Dreams are so weird.

But, anyway, in my dream, I just did it. I ran, and I sort of tripped forward, and then I was flying. I could turn over any way I liked, I could spin, I could just whoosh around. There was no friction to stop me.

Ice-skating is like flying.

I remember how hard it was at first. I kept looking at my feet, clunking around, trying to skate the same way I walked. It was only when I learned to look forward, and to glide instead of walk, that I could move the way I wanted to.

I tightened my laces the way I always do before I hit the ice — left skate first, then right, and both in double knots. I don't know why I go left to right on my ice skates. I do my shoes right to left. Anyway, I tightened them, then stepped forward onto the ice. I skated to the center, then waved at Ms. Mission.

The music started.

The notes from my grandmother's *tiple* fell over me like cool rain as I skated across the ice. I tried to concentrate on the music, to express how it made me feel using my movements. I thought about Lita, and how much my grandfather still missed her.

Before I knew it, I'd skated right into the axel, and landed it perfectly. I smiled to myself. *See? Don't think about it!*

I felt as if electricity was coursing through my body as I skated the rest of the program. The movements came by themselves — I didn't even have to try to remember them. It was as if the music was just making the movement happen. *This is what it's supposed to be like,* I realized. For the first time, my routine felt perfect.

At last, the final notes rang through the food court, blasting over the rink. I hit my pose, and the music stopped. A couple of people at the French bakery started to clap. Feeling light-headed and happy, I laughed and took a bow. Then I turned, and that was when I saw her.

"Meena!" I shouted and waved before I even registered the look on her face. Meena looked pale and shaken — as if someone had just slapped her.

Omigosh, I told Meena that I couldn't come to the mall with her today, I realized. *I told her that I was going to be with Jessica.*

And here I am.

"Meena!" I shouted again. "Wait!" I skated to the edge of the ice, but she had already turned away. She raced to the escalator and took the moving steps two by two. In a moment, she was out of sight.

Tears burned at the back of my eyes. As good as I was feeling before — that was how *bad* I was feeling now. I don't know why it hadn't occurred to me that Meena would go shopping without me.

I hadn't meant to hurt my friend's feelings, but I had.

But I'll get a chance to explain everything to her tonight, I told myself. *When we all go bowling.*

Meena won't think this is a big deal.

I hope.

Chapter Ten

R: Mandy told me the funniest story the other day! Give a call and I'll tell you.

xo, J

"What's your name?" Reggie asked me as he sat at the bowling lane's computer.

"Hmm? What?" I cocked my head. I was pretty sure I looked as confused as I felt. "Rosa."

Reggie laughed. "No, what's your *bowling* name?" Dance music was blaring all around us, and the bowling lanes had turned on a black light, which made the balls and pins glow with eerie neon colors. "You need a nickname to intimidate your opponent. Mine's the Cleaner."

"Mine's the Terminator," Anton announced, and Reggie typed it in.

"Strike Queen," Jacqui volunteered as she pulled on her red-and-blue bowling shoes. Amazingly, she was wearing an outfit that coordinated with those colors exactly — a red dress with red, blue, and black striped tights. I wondered if she planned it.

"Strike Queen isn't intimidating," Anton told her. "It should be, like, Strike Alien or something. Hairy, ugly Strike Alien."

Jacqui glared at her brother, who was grinning. I had to stifle a giggle.

"The Striker?" Reggie suggested.

"I'll stick with Strike Queen," Jacqui told him.

"I'll go with the Crusher," Carleton said.

That's appropriate, I thought. *Given how Meena feels about him.*

Reggie looked at me, eyebrows lifted.

"Um . . . I don't know, I can't think of anything," I confessed. I glanced over my shoulder, hoping to see Meena, but she was nowhere in sight. I felt my heart tighten. *Why isn't she here?* But I had a bad feeling that I knew why.

"How about Spare Girl?" Jacqui suggested with a smirk. "Just kidding!" she added, laughing at her own bowling pun. It only made me want to throttle her more.

Just picture her falling down when she tries to bowl, I told myself. It worked.

"Too bad Meena isn't here," Reggie said. "She's always good at coming up with names."

"Yeah. . . . Where is she?" Carleton asked. "Is she coming?"

I cringed a little bit.

"Supposed to be," Reggie told him. "Okay, Rosa. We've got to come up with something good for you."

"Just put down Spare Girl," I told him. That was how I was feeling, anyway.

"No way." Reggie tapped his fingers against the computer desk. "Got it!" He typed in SUPER BOWL, which made me laugh.

A cheery calypso beat chirped, and Reggie slapped his front pants pocket. He pulled out a cell phone and looked at the screen. "It's a text from Meena," he announced. "She can't make it — she feels sick."

"Is she okay?" Carleton asked. His eyebrows were drawn together in worry over his dark eyes.

"She probably just ate something weird," Jacqui said. She poked Carleton's shoulder. "She'll be fine."

I sank down in the orange vinyl booth. Of course, I knew the *real* reason Meena wasn't coming. It was true that she didn't feel good. She felt like she didn't want to hang out with Lousy Friend and Annoying Jacqui. And who could blame her?

"Too bad," Reggie said as he tucked the phone back into his pocket. "Meena's fun. And she's really good."

"Yeah," Carleton said softly.

"Okay, well, these balls aren't going to bowl themselves," Reggie said. "Who's first?"

"The Terminator," Anton announced. He stood up and grabbed a bright blue ball. He paused a moment to focus on the pins. Then he inhaled deeply, took three long steps, and unleashed the ball. It streaked over the glossy wood, spinning toward the pins. They exploded to either side — Anton had knocked them all over. "Yes!" he said, pumping his fist.

"Wow!" I was really impressed.

"Okay, my turn," Reggie said. He stood up and grabbed an orange ball. Then he walked up to the line and bent over in a half lean, half squat. He gave the ball a push, and it thunked onto the wood. Slowly, slowly, it rolled down the lane. As it neared the pins, it drifted slightly to the left. "Go right!" Reggie yelled. "Right!" He leaned to the left, as if balancing for the ball, which didn't go right, but at least managed to hang onto the edge of the lane. It knocked over two pins.

Reggie jumped. "Yeah!" He turned to Anton. "In your face!"

I completely cracked up.

Anton cocked an eyebrow at him. "You only knocked over two."

"The Cleaner is just getting started, baby," Reggie said. He grabbed another ball and rolled it just as he had the first. It landed in the gutter. "Okay, not my best effort," Reggie admitted as he sat down to record his score.

"Not your best effort?" Anton repeated. "Dude, you're the worst bowler on the planet!"

"It's a big planet," Reggie told him. He totally kept a straight face, but I couldn't.

After that, Carleton got up to bowl. He managed to hit seven pins in his two turns. Then it was Jacqui's turn, and she made a huge deal about asking Carleton for advice on her technique.

"How many steps do you take before you release the ball, Carleton?" Jacqui asked. "And do you focus on the center pin? Or do you focus on the ball?"

"Well — I'm not even really sure." Carleton laughed and shifted in his seat. "I just kind of — bowl."

Reggie flashed me a half-smile look and shook his head. Of course, if Jacqui really wanted bowling advice, the person to ask was *Anton*. But Carleton seemed completely clueless. Anton just munched a curly fry and rolled his eyes.

Jacqui knocked over eight pins, then it was my turn. The funny thing about bowling is that it's one sport that I don't mind being lousy at. I hate it when I strike out in baseball, and it makes me crazy when I can't get a basketball through the hoop. And I think we all know how I feel about falling down while ice-skating. *But a gutterball?* Big whoop.

I chose a neon-yellow ball. I took a few quick steps, and then let it go, trying to remember what Papi had taught me. He liked to play bocce ball — which is kind of like bowling. He said that you should always keep your arm straight and focus on a point a little beyond the ball. I knocked down six pins. Four were still standing on the left side.

"Good one!" Reggie said as I retrieved my ball.

"Take bigger steps," Anton volunteered. "You're taking a bunch of little steps."

"Okay," I said. I felt a weird mix of emotions as I grabbed the yellow ball and stood a few steps from the line. I was a little embarrassed that Anton didn't like my bowling technique. But I was kind of happy that he'd been paying attention. In the end, I decided that I should just take his advice, and not obsess over whether it meant anything. I took one, two, three steps and bowled.

At first, the ball went straight. Then Reggie

yelled at it. "Go left! Go left!" Weirdly, the ball actually seemed to listen to him, and it drifted toward the pins — and hit them!

"A spare!" I cried, flinging my hands in the air.

"All right!" Reggie held up a hand for a high five, and I smacked it. "I helped!"

I laughed. "You sure did!"

"Are you kidding? *I* helped," Anton put in.

"Also true," I told him.

"It was just luck." Jacqui snorted. She looked at Carleton, who shrugged.

"Rosa bowls better than I do," he said.

What a sweetie. For the millionth time, I wished Meena was here.

"You're an excellent bowler, Carleton," Jacqui told him.

Ugh. Seriously, now *I* was feeling sick to my stomach. *Maybe I have what Meena has.*

Anton went up and bowled his turn. He got a spare, which earned a fist-pump. He came and sat down beside me while Reggie got up to bowl. "So, Rosa, are you ready for the competition Monday?"

I rolled my eyes. "Define 'ready.'"

I expected Anton to laugh, but he didn't. "Jacqui's been practicing like crazy. Our mother has been coaching her." He sneaked a glance at his sister, who was on the booth across from ours, deep in conversation with Carleton.

"Your mother?" I repeated.

"Yeah. Didn't you know? She was on the Olympic team in the early 1990s."

"You're kidding. That's amazing!" Actually, I couldn't believe that Jacqui hadn't bragged about it.

Anton leaned back against the booth. "She was supposed to skate — but she injured her tendon. So the alternate got her shot."

"Oh."

"So she's really kind of . . . *intense* about skating," Anton explained. "Jacqui is, too."

"I guess it's genetic," I said.

Anton nodded. "Yeah. I guess."

He was so close that I could smell the sweet scent of his clean clothes. His green eyes held mine in a steady gaze, and I felt like I was holding my breath. "Anyway, if you want to beat her, you're going to have to work as hard as she does, that's all I'm saying," Anton went on.

"Yeah." I felt like one of those snakes that gets hypnotized by the flute player. If Anton would just keep talking, I would just sit here forever.

"So if you're not feeling ready, you should probably practice tomorrow," Anton said. He laid his arm against the back of the booth. It was right there, next to me. Like, kind of almost *around* me. "I know Jacqui's going to be practicing."

"What's this about tomorrow?" Reggie asked as he walked over to join us. "Rosa and I are heading over to the Field Museum."

Anton looked at me. "Why?"

Something about his glance made me squirm. "We're doing a project."

"We've got to check out some rocks." Reggie sat down at the computer and recorded his score: three.

"Rocks?" Anton looked as if we'd just told him we were going to check out nuclear waste. "Reggie, dude, Rosa has a competition on Monday. Did you know that?"

"Sure," Reggie said. He looked at me. "Is that a problem? Do you want to bag the museum?"

"No," I said quickly. Actually, I really didn't. Going to the museum actually sounded like fun.

"She's just being polite," Anton told Reggie. "She seriously needs to practice all day if she wants to win this thing." He turned to me. "You do want to win it, right?"

"Yeah, but —" I hesitated and sneaked a glance at Jacqui. *I do want to win, don't I?*

Reggie looked at me. I could tell he was trying to read my face. "It's not a big deal if you can't go," he said slowly. "I can check out the museum, and you can just do more research online or at the library. Then we can put everything together."

I heaved a sigh. Reggie's green eyes were warm and sweet. I could tell he really *wouldn't* mind if I didn't come along — he wasn't just saying it. It was really nice of him to volunteer to do that work for the both of us.

Just then, Jacqui let out a squeal. She'd just hit a strike.

"Nice one," Carleton called.

Jacqui turned and looked at me . . . and gave me this *smirk*.

"I think I'd better practice," I said to Reggie.

He nodded. "I totally understand."

Anton gave me a smile, then patted my arm. "It's your turn," he said.

At first, I thought he was talking about the competition — like, *Rosa, it's your turn to win*. But then I realized that he meant it was my turn to bowl.

It's my turn all right, I thought as I stood up. *Jacqui — watch out.*

Chapter Eleven

Rosa, Haven't heard from you. You aren't mad, R U?
J-Day

"Oof!" I skidded across the ice with my leg tucked under my body. It would have been a pretty cool move — if I'd been doing it on purpose. I struggled to my feet. For some reason, I just couldn't make the axel happen this morning.

Papi watched me from the chairs, calmly sipping his coffee. His dark eyes were bright, and I felt them following me as I skated toward him. He'd gotten up early to bring me to the mall, so I could practice. I explained I planned to stay all day, and I'd told him that he could just leave me here. But he refused. He wanted to stay and watch for a while, he said.

My grandmother's *tiple* played on as I clomped off the ice and plopped into the chair beside Papi. I didn't say anything, but I felt the tears burning at the back of my eyes. I had the jump yesterday — why couldn't I get it today? This extra practice was supposed to be *helping*, not setting me back.

Papi closed his eyes and hummed along with the familiar music. "Ah, I love to hear this music," he said. "And to see you skate to it — I feel like the luckiest man."

My smile was wry. "Yeah, you're so lucky that you get to watch me fall over."

Papi looked surprised. "This is only practice," he said. "You're supposed to fall in practice."

"But the competition is tomorrow!"

"Ah, yes. Well, perhaps you have practiced enough."

"How can you say that? I keep falling!"

Papi took a long pull from the sip top of his coffee. "Well, your grandmother used to say that music is like cooking. If you fuss with it too much, it doesn't seem fresh."

"So — wait — maybe I'm practicing too much?"

"Maybe."

"But how do I know if it's too much, or not enough?"

Papi turned to look at me full in the face. "Do you feel that you *want* to practice more?"

"No."

"Hmm." Papi closed his eyes. I started to say something, but he held up his hand. "Hush. This is my favorite part." The *tiple* music fluttered and soared. After a few moments, the music was over. Slowly, Papi opened his eyes. I saw that there were tears in them. "So beautiful," he murmured.

"It really is," I agreed. I'd always loved this recording, but over the days that I had been skating to it, I'd really started to appreciate it in a whole new way. "Why didn't Lita become a professional musician? Mom says she could have."

Papi stared out at the ice. He seemed to be thinking it over. "Yes, she could have."

"Didn't she want to?"

"Your grandmother played for money a few times. This was before we were married. She played in a restaurant, and people gave her tips. She hated it. She said that it made playing the *tiple* feel like a job. If people didn't tip very much, she felt that she hadn't played well. She woke up and dreaded having to go to work." Papi sipped his coffee thoughtfully.

For a moment, I thought he wasn't going to say anything else. Then he went on, "Lita played the *tiple* because she loved it. She loved bringing joy to others. But she didn't feel that it had to be her job. So she got another job. She became a librarian — which she also loved. And she didn't have to worry that nobody would give her a tip, because nobody tips librarians."

"I guess I can see that," I said after a moment. "She played the *tiple* for fun. The money took the fun out of it."

"Exactly." Papi smiled. "That is what your mother never understood. She always felt that Lita should have tried to be a virtuoso. Karin never understood that your grandmother didn't have that kind of ambition. Karin is ambitious, of course. And that's good. She has been very successful, and makes a lot of money, and inspires a lot of people. But your grandmother just wanted a simple life. And that's good, too."

We sat in silence for a little while.

"So," Papi said after a moment, "are you going to get back out there?" He waved his paper coffee cup in the direction of the ice.

I sighed. *I should,* I told myself. *I should if I want to beat Jacqui.* But I just couldn't make myself get up.

"Papi, would you mind dropping me off at the Field Museum?" I asked at last. "I've got to work on this project."

Papi touched my chin with gentle fingers. "Of course, *amorcita*," he said. "Whatever makes you happy."

Reggie didn't spot me right away. He was peering into a case, then scribbling madly in a notebook. It was fun to stand there and just watch him for a minute. His expression was really intense, as if the gem in the case was the most important thing in the world. Or maybe the only thing in the world.

I walked over and tapped him on the shoulder.

"Rosa!" Reggie cried when he saw me. He gave me a huge smile and wrapped me in a warm hug. I was so surprised that, for a moment, I didn't hug back.

"Um, hey." I patted Reggie on the back.

Reggie backed away, blushing a little. He shuffled his feet and jammed a hand in his pocket. He cleared his throat, then gave me an embarrassed smile. "Whoa — that was weird, right? I mean —" He laughed. "Where did that come from?"

His embarrassment made me smile. "No, it was nice," I told him, and I really meant it. "Actually, I kind of needed a hug. You just surprised me."

Reggie ran a hand through his hair. "So . . . uh . . . you made it! I wasn't expecting you."

"Yeah, I just couldn't deal with practicing for another second," I admitted.

"Sometimes you've studied enough."

"I guess."

Reggie gave me a friendly punch in the arm. "You're ready," he told me.

I didn't know what to say to that. "Yeah, you're right," sounded arrogant, and "No, I'm not," sounded lame, so I just stood there awkwardly for another moment until Reggie rescued me.

"So, I've been looking at these diamonds. . . ." Reggie said. We were standing in the Grainger Hall of Gems, surrounded by beautiful, polished stones. Some of them were in elaborate jewelry settings.

"Wow, look at that mermaid," I said, pointing to a gorgeous stained-glass window nearby. We walked over to take a closer look. The window was done in shades of green and blue, and seemed to glow as the light filtered through it. A mermaid was looking up at a yellow fish, and little bubbles floated up around them.

"Yeah. Have you heard of Tiffany and Company?" Reggie asked.

"The jewelry maker?" I asked.

"Right. Charles Lewis Tiffany founded the company. Well, a lot of the gems here were his. And the window was made by his son."

"I wonder what their house was like."

Reggie laughed. "Probably pretty nice."

"How do you know all that stuff about the Tiffanys?" I asked.

Reggie blushed a little. "I've been here before."

"Like a million times?"

"Maybe two million," he admitted. "It's a cool museum."

We walked around a little while. I pulled out my camera and snapped a few photos of the gems. They had everything — from rocks that looked like they had just been pulled out of the ground to stones that had been cut by masters. "We might want to talk about how the crystals form, and the way that they can be cut to catch the light."

"I was thinking the same thing," Reggie agreed. "Ms. Fontayne likes it when you include graphs and stuff, so maybe we could add in some comparisons between stone hardness, brilliance, and the way the crystal forms."

"Sounds good. Holy moly!" I crossed over to a gem the size of a grapefruit. It was pale blue, and teardrop shaped. "Is that a diamond?"

"It's a topaz," Reggie told me. "It weighs two and a half pounds. They can get really big."

"Crazy." We walked around the hall a little while. "They're all so beautiful. I think that's the most beautiful thing I've ever seen." I pointed to a large emerald surrounded by small rectangular diamonds set in a white gold pendant.

Reggie lifted his eyebrows. "That's your favorite?" he asked.

"Well, it's hard to pick a favorite," I admitted. "But that one's up there. What's yours?"

He looked around. "This one," he said, walking over to a case. Inside was a giant chunk of white rock. Cloudy red stones poked out of it.

"What is that?" I asked.

"Rubies," Reggie said. "Just the crystals. They're still stuck in the marble. Nobody's polished them up yet."

"You like them all natural, huh?"

Reggie shrugged. "They're just being themselves. They're still beautiful. They don't need anyone to fix them. And each one is unique. No one's carved them up to make them into something else."

I looked at the rock. "True," I admitted. "But this would make a pretty lousy necklace." I mean, the thing must have weighed five pounds.

Reggie laughed. "Good point."

I smiled at him, and actually felt my body relax a little. I checked my watch, and my jaw dropped nearly to the floor. We'd been looking around for an hour and a half! "Wow!" I said. "I actually managed to go, like, forty minutes without thinking about skating."

"That's good — right?" Reggie asked.

"Yeah, that's good."

"Just go out there and have fun tomorrow," Reggie said.

I laughed. "Aren't I supposed to win?"

Reggie cocked his head. "You tell me," he said.

I thought about it. "Well, I hope I do."

"Okay," Reggie said.

Something in his gaze made me feel warm inside. *Just go out there and have fun.*

What a concept.

When I got home, I immediately noticed that something was wrong: Amelia wasn't in my room, demanding that I entertain her. She wasn't waiting for me in the living room either. She wasn't snacking on breakfast cereal in the kitchen.

"Amelia?" I called.

I heard something. It sounded like a sniffle. And it was coming from Amelia's room, of all places.

I knocked gently on the closed door. "Amelia?"

There was no answer, but I heard another sniffle.

I knocked again.

"Go away."

"Are you okay?" I asked.

"I'm fine!" she shouted in a way that didn't sound very fine to me.

I hesitated, unsure what to do. I didn't want to pressure her. But I didn't want to just leave either. *Maybe she just needs a little push . . . or maybe she just needs to be alone for a while. . . .*

"Are you still there?" Amelia asked after a moment.

"Yes."

"Well, go away. I'm perfectly fine all by my" — Amelia's voice broke a little — "self." *Sniffle*. Then I heard sobbing.

I opened the door a crack and peeked inside. She had flung herself across her bed, and was lying facedown with her head almost buried in pillows. She was wearing a gray shirt and dark jeans, and she looked like a small rainstorm against her fluffy pale blue comforter covered in white clouds.

I walked over to her bed and perched at the foot. I touched her back — which was heaving with sobs. "You don't seem fine," I said gently.

Amelia muttered something into her pillow. I pulled it away from her face. "What?"

"Of course I'm not fine!" Amelia wailed. "I'm miserable! Isn't it obvious?"

"Um, yes?"

Amelia sat up and took a deep, shuddering breath. Her eyes were red, and her face was pale and blotchy. Her hair was wild around her face, and I smoothed it back, tucking a lock behind her ear. Look, my sister may be a drama queen, but she doesn't cry that much, so I knew that whatever was bothering her was something real. Something important. "Do you want to talk about it?"

My sister looked up at me with her wide hazel eyes. "Molly's party was yesterday," she said. Her voice was a hoarse whisper.

"Oh," I said, a realization settling over me like a heavy weight. The party was yesterday — and Amelia hadn't been invited.

Amelia had to swallow hard before she could speak. "When I didn't get an invitation, I thought she would call, or something. . . . But she never did."

"That's — awful."

Amelia picked at one of the tassels on her blue pillow. "It's just so . . . mean. I thought we were friends." And the way she said "friends" made my heart feel as if it was going to split in two.

"Oh, Amelia." I took her hand, and she rested her head against my shoulder. I patted her hair. "The same thing happened to me. Well, sort of."

Amelia lifted her eyebrows.

"Jessica said she was coming for a visit," I admitted. "Then she bagged at the last minute."

Amelia snorted. "Well, that's not surprising," she said. "Jessica's always been a flake."

"What?" I pulled away to stare at my sister. "No she isn't."

"Oh, please. What about that time she left you waiting at the entrance to the mall for half an hour, and then showed up with three girls you didn't even know?"

I'd forgotten all about that.

"And the time she bagged on going to the movie at the last minute because she 'didn't feel well' — and then you heard she was over at Natalie's house two hours later, eating pizza and watching movies?"

"Why do you remember all of this stuff better than I do?" I asked.

"I don't know."

Amelia was right, though. Jessica had flaked out loads of times. I guess I'd always just thought

153

that it was "Jessica being Jessica." But now I was starting to wonder — maybe she was always just kind of a lousy friend.

"Friends don't just bail on each other for no good reason," Amelia said. "I mean, we're supposed to stick together, right?"

I winced, thinking about Meena's face when she saw me ice-skating. "Yeah," I admitted, "friends are supposed to stick together."

Amelia sighed. "So, what am I going to do? I don't want to go back to school."

"You need a new friend," I told her.

Amelia laughed bitterly. "Okay. Well, I'll have Mom drop me off at the grocery store. Maybe I can pick one up."

"No, I'm serious," I said. "Look, isn't there anyone else in your class who you want to get to know? Anyone who seems nice?"

Amelia bit her lip. "Well . . . there is this one girl. Laura. She's really quiet and sits in the back. But Ms. Jensen paired us up to work together the other day, and Laura was really funny."

"Why don't you ask if she wants to come to the skating competition tomorrow?" I asked. "You guys could hang out at the mall for a while afterward."

"What if she says no?" Amelia asked.

"Then you'll be in the same boat you're in now."

Amelia hesitated. "I don't know. . . ."

"It's hard, I know," I told her. "Just — think about it, okay?"

Amelia nodded. "Okay."

I was about to get up when Amelia surprised me by throwing her arms around me. It was my second surprise hug of the day. But this time, I was more prepared.

I made sure to hug back.

Chapter Twelve

hi, rosie! dad has to go to chicago again next month —
so cu then! thx for understanding about the dance. it
was gr8, btw! have lots of stories for u. (hint: mandy and
erin t. aren't speaking!)

   lv, j-day

I read the e-mail three times, trying to decide how
to respond. My talk with Amelia had opened my
eyes about Jessica, and now I just couldn't close
them and go back to feeling the same way about

her that I used to. *Jessica's always been a flake,* Amelia had said.

Yeah, I guess she was. Only before, I was used to it. In just a month of living in Chicago, I'd forgotten what Jessica was like.

So I didn't really want her to come to Chicago for a visit. And I couldn't imagine anything I wanted to hear less than a story about Mandy and Erin T. I didn't even know who Erin T. *was.* But did I even need to write and tell "J-Day" how I felt? She'd probably just bag on our plans at the last minute, anyway.

And P.S., J-Day: I don't *understand about the dance.*

"Grr." I clicked the e-mail closed and checked my buddy list. Meena was online.

A slithery, slimy feeling came over me from my insides, as if someone had just poured toxic goo down my throat. *You're mad at Jessica, but you did the same thing to Meena,* I thought.

I was supposed to be working on my earth science makeup homework, but I couldn't focus. Instead, I squirmed in my chair, feeling like an absolute jerk. Without thinking, my fingers flew over the keys.

myammeegirl: U there?

The refrigerator hummed, the only noise in the kitchen. I felt time ticking away. Meena didn't respond. But I had a feeling that she hadn't just stepped away from the computer. I felt like she was reading that message the way I'd read Jessica's — wondering what to do with it.

myammeegirl: Missed u at bowling.

The cursor blinked on and off, on and off. Still no reply. Okay, maybe she really wasn't there. I decided to try one more time.

myammeegirl: Carleton seemed really disappointed.

Blink. Blink.

shadowknows: Really?

I smiled. I crossed the kitchen and grabbed the cordless off the wall. For what I had to say, IM just wasn't going to cut it. I punched in Meena's number and waited.

She picked up after two rings. "Hey," she said.

"He was totally disappointed," I told her. "And Jacqui kept trying to get his attention, but he was not into her at all."

For a moment, Meena didn't say anything. "Who is this?" she asked.

"Meena!" I screeched. "It's me — Rosa!"

"Just *kidding*," she said. "I have caller ID, like everyone else in the world. So, like, did he say anything about me?"

I could almost feel her blushing through the phone line. "Well . . . he was worried when he heard you were sick. And when Reggie said you were really fun, he agreed."

"He thinks I'm fun?" Meena asked in a small voice.

"Meena, everybody thinks you're fun. You're, like, fun in human form."

Meena sighed. Silence lingered on the line.

"Listen, Meena, I just wanted to say I'm really sorry about Saturday. I just — I don't know. My friend canceled on me at the last minute, and then

I felt like I needed to practice more, and I guess this whole competition has just warped my brain, or something, because I don't know why I didn't hang out with you that day. I'm *so* sorry."

"It's okay," Meena said slowly. "It's just — I was feeling really nervous that day. . . ."

"I know." My fingers gripped the receiver. "I know."

"And then I really *did* feel sick that night," Meena went on. "My stomach was killing me. But I'm better now."

"Carleton will be relieved to hear it."

Meena giggled. Then she said, "Thanks, Rosa. And thanks for saying you're sorry. I was really . . ." She didn't finish her sentence, but I knew what she meant. She was sad, because we were getting to be good friends.

"Yeah," I said. "Me too."

"So, uh . . ." Meena cleared her throat. "Did Carleton say anything else about me?"

"Let me think."

Just then, I heard a banging, and someone shouted a muffled "Meena!"

"Go away, Tarik!" Meena called. "It's just one of

my dumb brothers," she said to me. "Ignore the pounding."

"Dinner's ready, you goober! If you don't come down, I'm eating your aloo gobi!"

"Oh, Mom made my favorite," Meena said. "Gotta go, or my greedy siblings will gobble it all up!"

"Okay, I'll see you tomorrow."

"Oh, right! Tomorrow! I forgot all about the competition," Meena said.

"Seriously?"

"Well — kind of. I just wasn't thinking about it." Meena laughed. "I'm sure I would have remembered in time to show up."

I laughed and said good-bye. Wow. She just kind of — spaced on the competition. For me, I felt like it was always hovering just outside my mind, like some kind of greedy bird, waiting to pick at the bones of my thoughts.

Well, at least tomorrow, it will all be over, I thought. *Either way, it will be over.*

For some reason, I wasn't relieved.

I turned over my spoonful of oatmeal and watched as it plopped back into my bowl.

"That's for eating, not playing with," my mother told me.

I sighed. "I'm just not hungry."

She looked up from her newspaper. "You've got to eat before the competition." Mom walked over to the counter for a refill of her coffee. "You can't skate on an empty stomach."

I knew that she was right. I mean, I didn't want to fall over in the middle of free skate. Then again, this oatmeal was yucking me out. It's usually one of my favorite things to have for breakfast — that was why Mom made it for me. But I just couldn't seem to work up an appetite for it.

Something stomped and thudded down the stairs. A moment later, my little sister danced into the kitchen, humming a pop tune. *"Yeah, yeah, ye-ah,"* she sang as she bopped over to the counter. *"There's a party goin' on right now."* Amelia waggled her hips and poured cereal into a bowl. She bumped her hip against Mom's, then dropped into the chair across from mine.

Mom laughed. "You're in a good mood."

"Yep." Amelia took a huge spoonful of cereal and crunched it, grinning.

"Why so smiley?" I asked her. Actually, I couldn't

help smiling myself. I hadn't realized how much I'd missed the "old" Amelia until she showed up again.

"No reason. I just can't wait to see you win today," Amelia said.

"Don't jinx me!" I rapped my knuckles against the wooden table. "That's bad luck."

"You don't need luck," Amelia said, and I swear, I wanted to hug her. "That's what my new friend, Laura, always says. She's coming to the competition today, by the way." Amelia peeked up at me, shyly.

"Laura — from class?" I asked. Amelia nodded and I smiled. So Amelia *had* asked her. I was glad.

"What happened to Molly?" Mom put in.

"Who?" Amelia asked innocently. Then she winked at me and went on humming.

"How's my skater girl?" Papi rubbed his papery hands together as he walked into the kitchen. "I have a surprise for you!"

"What is it?" I asked.

Papi batted his eyelashes in this Gee Whiz I Don't Know kind of way and rolled his shoulders. "Hmm. Maybe you should go look in your room."

Mom's eyebrows were lifted, but she was staring into her coffee with this tiny little smile, as if she knew what was coming. I knew it had to be my new skating dress, and a tiny stab of fear darted through me. No matter what it looked like, I knew I'd have to wear it. Even if it looked like a wedding cake. Even if it was made out of burlap.

Amelia had started humming crazily again and was wiggling around in her chair as if she might just bust into a break dance at any moment.

My chair squeaked loudly as I pushed it away from the table. I smiled nervously at Papi, who was beaming as I made my way out of the kitchen. The two bites of oatmeal that I'd eaten sat like a boulder in my stomach as I trudged up the narrow stairs to my room.

I pushed open the door to my room, and there it was: Laid out across my bed was a beautiful, white skating dress. It sparkled with a slight silver shimmer, and there were silver beads at the hem, cuff, and scooped neck. I let out a little whoop and rushed over to hold it up against my body. When I looked in the mirror, I saw that the white made my black hair and dark eyes look even brighter.

"Oh, it's gorgeous!" I said to Papi, who had just appeared in my doorway. "I love it!" I rushed over to give him a warm hug.

Papi rested his cheek against the top of my head. "You will look like a snowflake, eh?"

"It's just perfect," I whispered against his scratchy sweater.

"Lemme see, lemme see!" Amelia grabbed the dress out of my hands. "Oooh! So pretty! Papi, can I have one, too?"

"You don't even ice-skate," I pointed out.

Amelia looked at me as if I were crazy. "So?"

"It's really lovely, Papa," Mom said. She put a gentle hand on his shoulder. Papi put his wrinkled, old hand over hers.

"Put it on!" Amelia urged.

"Not yet," I told her.

"It's getting late," Mom said. "You'll need to get dressed soon. We have to be at the rink in half an hour."

"I know, but I don't want to spill food on it. I've got to eat breakfast!" Suddenly, I was completely ravenous.

"Ah — see?" Papi smiled. "The athlete has a good appetite!"

"Okay, eat up, so you can win!" Amelia crowed.

"Stop saying that!" I cried.

"Okay, okay — I'll stop." Amelia scrunched up her face into an evil grin. "As soon as you *win*!"

I clapped my hands over my ears. "I can't hear you!" I hollered, but I was laughing.

"Win! Win! Win!" Amelia shouted as she raced down the stairs after me.

I could hear her voice ringing in my ears all the way to the rink.

Chapter Thirteen

shadowknows: Just wanted to say good luck.

myammeegirl: You too, Meena!

shadowknows: You're going to be great.

myammeegirl: I hope so.

shadowknows: Believe it.

myammeegirl: :-D

"There are more than I thought there would be," Atlanta said as she surveyed the crowded ice. Girls from all over Chicago were warming up, practicing spins and jumps, and looking generally intense and nervous.

"Some of them are really good," I said as a dark-haired girl nailed a combination and moved into a standing spin. My heart thudded in my chest. For weeks, I'd been thinking of Jacqui as my only competition. I was just starting to realize that the city was *full* of good skaters. I felt confidence leaking out of me like a dripping faucet.

Meena skated up to us and skidded to a stop. "Whoa! Did you see that girl who just pulled off a triple jump?"

I *had* seen it. It had filled me with horror.

"She's amazing!" Meena's face was lit up, like she'd just seen an incredible fireworks display or something.

"Doesn't that make you *nervous*?" I asked her.

Meena looked surprised. "What do I care?" she asked. "I'm not going to win, anyway."

"Don't say that!" Atlanta gave Meena a gentle punch in the arm.

"Why not? It's not like I'm putting myself down, or something. It's just true." Meena shrugged. "I'm lucky — I can just try to do my best. I don't have to worry, like Rosa does."

Atlanta looked offended.

"And like *you* do!" Meena added quickly.

Atlanta sighed. "No, you're right. I'm just shooting for the top ten, not the podium."

"Well, if I want to be in the top three, I guess I'd better start warming up," I said. I'd stretched out earlier, but five minutes near the ice had made my muscles cold. I skated three laps around the rink to get my blood flowing again. I practiced my spins, then moved into a single toe loop. Every single time I land a jump, I feel like I've just won a race. Like I've just done something amazing.

I moved on to the axel. I did it once. Then I went around to do it again. Then one more time. The last time was the best. I landed so solidly, I felt like I was standing still on two feet and flying at the same time. It felt beautiful, like wearing a gorgeous dress. *I've got it.*

Then I had this weird feeling that if I tried it again, I'd wreck the whole thing, so I hung back and watched the other skaters for a while.

I caught a movement out of the corner of my eye, and when I looked, I saw Anton waving at me. A wave of heat shot through me — I'm surprised the ice didn't start melting beneath my feet. I skated over to say hello, blushing all the way.

"Just got here," Anton said as I skated up to him. "My mom spent about two hours on Jacqui's hair." He rolled his eyes.

I laughed and looked over to where Jacqui was pulling on her skates. Her hair was back in a tight bun, with a diamond tiara around it. "Wow. I can see why." In her orange-and-yellow dress studded with crystals, she looked like a fairy princess. Queen of the Fall Leaves or something.

"You look great," Anton said, and I felt a goofy grin take over my face.

"Thanks."

"I sure hope you practiced enough." Anton shook his head. "Otherwise it won't matter how good you look."

Whoa. My goofy grin sure disappeared in a hurry. "Aren't you supposed to tell me good luck, or something?"

Anton cocked his head. "The best skater is going to win. It's not about luck."

Somehow, it had sounded really different when Amelia said it. I guess because she sounded so sure that I was the best skater.

Anton watched the other girls warm up. "Pretty different from Miami, right? I bet the skaters here are way better."

I gritted my teeth. Okay, what he was saying was true. It just wasn't what I wanted to hear at that moment. It was the *way* he said it, I think. Suddenly, I wanted to get away from Anton before I heard anything else that would sink my confidence.

Just then, Reggie bounced over to us. "Hey, Rosa!" He patted my shoulder. "Go knock 'em out!" His green eyes were shining.

My shoulder felt warm beneath Reggie's fingers, and when I smiled at him, I felt my whole body relax. "Thanks, Reggie."

The public address system crackled. "Figure skaters, please take your seats. We are about to begin."

I skated over to where my friends had gathered. Meena patted the seat beside hers, and I sat down.

Ms. O'Malley was pacing, looking nervous. "Okay, everyone," she said in a low voice. "Just concentrate on skating your best, all right? It's not about winning. It's about *skating*. Got it?"

I heard Jacqui give a little snort behind me. Clearly, she thought it *was* all about winning. Not that I was surprised. Jacqui thought that *practice* was all about winning. She thought *everything* was all about winning.

I felt a tap on my shoulder, and Jacqui leaned forward, so that her face was between mine and Meena's. "Good luck, you two!" she chirped. "Did you see that Carleton is in the stands? He brought me a *rose!*" Jacqui giggled a little and sat back in her seat.

I looked up into the stands. Carleton was there. And he did have a purple rose in his lap. I felt Meena sink a little. Wow. Count on Jacqui to cut the string on your kite.

I took Meena's hand in mine and squeezed. She gave me a grateful look and smiled. "No big deal," she murmured.

"Liar," I said.

"I know," Meena agreed.

I looked out in the stands and caught sight of Papi and Mom. Amelia was with them munching on a giant pretzel and chatting with a tall girl. *Laura*, I supposed. As if she could feel my glance, Amelia looked over. She waved, and gave me a thumbs-up.

I waved back.

"Go, Rosa!" she shouted — it rang out through the entire mall. Everyone in the stands cracked up.

I wasn't sure whether to die of embarrassment, or crack up, too. But then the Zamboni pulled off the ice, and the announcer came on again. "Our skaters will first perform their short program. Our first skater is Leslie Armstrong," she announced.

And that was it. We were on our way.

I felt kind of sorry for the first skater as she took the ice — but mostly, I was just glad that I wasn't the one who had to go first. She was very small, and she was wearing a pretty purple dress with crystals across the top. Then her short program music started. She skated to an upbeat 50s-style song.

"Ooooh!" Meena clapped as the skater completed a single axel.

I elbowed her.

"What? She's really good!" Meena's eyes were shining.

I just laughed. It was true — she was really good. That was why it was making me sick to watch her.

I didn't feel sorry for her anymore. The judges gave her a 5.5, 5.3, and a 5.4. I thought that was kind of low — she had been really good.

"They're tough," Meena whispered, nodding at the judges.

"That just means they'll be tough on everyone," Atlanta pointed out.

Four more skaters performed their short programs. Lucky for me, none of them were that great. Then Jacqui took the ice.

I looked over at Meena, whose eyes were squeezed shut. "Are you okay?" I asked.

"No," Meena said. "I'm a horrible person."

"What? Why?"

Meena looked at me with huge brown eyes. "I just really want her to fall on her face."

I smiled and touched her hand. "I forgive you."

Jacqui struck her opening pose. From the moment her music started, I could tell that she was in the zone. For her short program, she had chosen a pretty ballad from a Broadway show, and her expression was spot on. Meena actually gasped as Jacqui nailed a double toe loop, and then burst into applause.

"I thought you wanted her to fall!" I teased.

"But that was so *amazing*!" Meena cried, still clapping.

I had to admit it was true. I was sitting at the edge of my seat as I watched Jacqui perform. If I could have just forgotten it was her, I would have really loved it.

When she was finished, the judges gave her a 5.8, 5.6, and 5.6. Jacqui frowned from her seat when she saw the scores, but I was glad. *Not unbeatable,* I told myself.

Six more skaters did their short programs, including Atlanta and Meena. Atlanta skated well — but, as usual, she was a little stiff. Meena wobbled a lot when she hit her jumps, but she didn't fall.

"Whew, glad that's over," she said as she dropped into the chair beside mine. "Now I can relax until the free skate."

Two more skaters, then it was my turn. I expected to be nervous when I skated out to the center ice — all those people watching me. But, somehow, having an audience made me feel calmer. I knew that Mom and Papi and Amelia were in that crowd, sending good vibes. I knew that Meena would clap her fingers off the minute I did anything halfway decent. And then my music started.

For the short program, I'd picked a piece of salsa music that had been popular at my school back in Miami. It made me smile to skate to it, which was good. I was supposed to be smiling, according to Ms. O'Malley.

The music picked up tempo, and so did I as I moved across the ice. I leaped into a spin, and heard clapping as I spun down to the ice, then moved back up again. I nailed a leap and then a spin. Another jump, and the music slowed slightly. One turn, then straight into a double. And in a few moments, my routine was over.

The spectators cheered as I skated toward my teammates. I saw Meena and Atlanta jumping up and down, yelling.

"That was great!" Meena said, thumping me on the back.

"Really? It felt good," I told her.

"Very nice," Atlanta said.

I sat down and waited for the judges' scores. Finally, they held up their cards: 5.6, 5.6, 5.8.

Meena gasped. "You're tied with Jacqui!"

"But that other girl is in first place," Atlanta pointed out. "The one in blue. Her name's Denise, I think."

"What?" Meena screeched. We all looked over at Denise, who was wearing a simple blue dress. She was sitting calmly beside her coach lightly tracing her finger against one of her skate blades and watching the Zamboni smooth the ice.

"Her dress isn't half as pretty as yours," Delia put in. "She should lose."

"It's not a fashion show," Meena said.

"It should be!" Delia huffed.

"Denise has got two five-eights," Atlanta explained. "That puts her point two ahead of you."

Meena's eyes narrowed and she clapped me on the shoulder. "You can still win it," she said.

For some reason, my heart was hammering in my chest and I felt like I was going blind in my left eye. I felt like I was about to get a visit from that morning's oatmeal. Time slowed down and sped up all at once. Meena was talking to me, but I had trouble focusing on the words. They came at me as if we were underwater — blurry, and hard to understand. Meanwhile, before I knew it, the

Zamboni had slid back into its lair, and the ice was cleared for the first skater — Denise.

She took the ice as if she was the queen of it. *I wish I had half of her confidence,* I thought. And then the music started.

"I can't watch." I squeezed my eyes shut.

Meena gasped, then burst into applause.

"What? What?" I opened my eyes to see Denise skating fluidly into a choctaw.

"Double axel," Meena whispered. "Gorgeous."

I covered my eyes again. "Don't tell me. And don't make any more noises!"

Meena gasped again, and I heard the crowd groan.

"What? What did I miss?"

"I thought you didn't want to know," Atlanta said.

"Don't listen to me!" I insisted.

"She put her hand on the ice during the sit spin," Meena explained.

Atlanta nodded knowingly. "Major point deductions."

Denise's smile had disappeared — her expression was grim, as if she were grinding her teeth. Her next jump was an easy one — a lutz — but she cheated it, coming off the inside edge of her skate.

"A flutz!" Meena gasped.

Atlanta nodded knowingly. "That'll cost her."

By the time Denise's free skate was over, she looked like she was about to cry. Suddenly, my nerves disappeared, and I just felt bad for her.

"Two five-threes and a five-oh," Atlanta said when the judges delivered their scores.

Meena winced. "Ouch."

Atlanta shrugged. "Not as bad as it could've been. But she'll be lucky to be in the top ten."

I watched impatiently as the other skaters went through their routines. It was even hard to pay attention while Meena was skating. But I forced myself — and I was glad that I did. She was grinning when she came off the ice.

"That's amazing!" Meena said when the judges revealed her marks: a 5.2, a 5.3, and a 5.2. She hugged me. "My best ever!"

"Fantastic!" I squeezed her back. She had skated a clean program, and her marks would have been higher if her jumps had been more challenging. "Next time, you'll win this thing!"

Meena rolled her eyes and smiled.

"You're in fifteenth," Atlanta told her.

"Wow, you're good at math," Meena said.

Atlanta was in thirteenth place before she skated her program, and ninth after. Then it was Jacqui's turn.

I had seen this free skate a hundred times — maybe a thousand. But I'd never seen Jacqui put so much of herself into it before. It was as if being in front of an audience brought out an added spark in her skating. And she really did look like a falling leaf blown by a playful wind as she skipped and danced across the ice.

Meena nudged me. "Now *you're* the one clapping!"

I looked down at my hands. She was right — Jacqui had just landed a gorgeous combination. "I guess I couldn't help myself."

But when it was all over, Jacqui's "performance smile" disappeared. She didn't look up at the audience, which was full of people clapping and shouting. Her face was a mask of stone as she skated to the boards.

"Great job, Jacqui," I said as she passed by us to take her seat.

She didn't hear me. I think she was just on some other planet.

Jacqui stared tensely at the judges until they revealed their scores: 5.9, 5.8, 5.8. The crowd went wild! Ms. O'Malley hugged Jacqui, who started to cry.

"What's she bawling about?" Atlanta demanded. "She's in first place!"

"She's relieved," I said, half to myself. For the first time, I realized just how much pressure it was to be Jacqui.

And I could relate.

"You can still beat her," Atlanta said.

My heart was fluttering against my chest like a bird beating its wings against a cage. After an excruciating wait, it was finally my turn.

Meena squeezed my hand. "You can do it," she whispered.

You can do it. Sure — I just had to skate a perfect program.

I heard the ice crunch slightly beneath my blades as I skated out to the center of the rink. There were a hundred voices in my head, all trying to talk at once.

"Win! Win! Win!"

"Just go out there and have fun."

"You can do it."

"You can still beat her."

"Win! Win! Win!"

The crowd went silent around me, and I felt the quiet like a warm blanket. The voices in my mind went soft as the music started to play. My grandmother's *tiple* filled the air, like snowflakes falling softly in a quiet forest. I tried to remember what Ms. O'Malley said — show expression, take up as much of the ice as you can, reach through your body, extend.

Remember it all, and keep skating, keep smiling.

Mohawk turn . . . keep smiling . . . single lutz (arms tight) and then I set the pick. . . .

I heard the crowd gasp before I realized what had happened. I looked down. I was sitting on the ice.

It's over, I realized.

My heart stopped, and a cold chill of horror washed over me. I'd fallen.

You lost, I thought. *You lost, you lost, you lost.*

My grandmother's music played on.

What are you going to do now?

And before I knew what I was doing, I got back up.

It seemed like forever, but it all happened in less than a heartbeat. I soared around the rink and hit a split jump. The crowd erupted into applause, and I felt myself smile. I spun into my camel spin, feeling the world tilt and whirl around me. I felt like a top.

My grandmother's *tiple* played, and I tried to reach for the meaning behind the notes. I'd never known my grandmother, but in those moments out on the ice, I felt like I was talking to her. As if — through her music — I could hear what she was trying to say. She was saying, "Don't worry. Just do what you love. Awards mean nothing. This is for *you*."

And, with my skating, I was telling her, *I understand*.

I leaped into a double lutz. The crowd cheered, and I felt a grin welling up from my toes. I spread my arms and pulled my leg into the hair-splitter. And then — instantly, almost magically — it was all over.

The crowd was on their feet. I felt their cheers wash over me like a wave as I smiled up into the stands. Mom and Papi were clapping and whistling. Amelia was jumping up and down — and so was her new friend. And a few rows behind them, Reggie cheered and waved his arms over his head.

I smiled up at him. *Just go out there and have fun,* he'd said. And I had. I flashed him a thumbs-up.

He flashed one back, and the warmth from his smile was enough to scare away the chill from the ice.

I knew the score wouldn't show it, but I knew I'd just skated a personal best.

I'd lost, but I felt like I'd won.

"Third," Atlanta said to me once the final skater left the ice. "You came in third. Jacqui won it."

I felt the name "Jacqui" land on me like a brick. Suddenly, all the good I'd been feeling evaporated, like steam off a bowl of soup.

Meena put an arm around me. "You still get a medal."

I tried to let that make me feel better, but it only worked a little. Now that it was final, I felt the weight of what it meant to come really, really close . . . and fail. "But I lost."

"Yeah," Atlanta said, tugging at her lower lip thoughtfully. "Losing always stinks."

"But you had the prettiest dress," Delia put in.

That actually made me smile. "I'll tell Papi that *he* won."

"Besides, none of us won either," Meena pointed out. "Atlanta — you got the best score out of the rest of us. What place are you in?"

Atlanta looked down at her feet, suddenly shy. "Seventh."

"Seventh?" Meena shrieked. "That's awesome!"

"Delia's in eleventh," Atlanta said. "And Meena — you came in fourteenth."

"Fourteenth?" Meena's eyes bugged out of her head. "*Fourteenth?* How many skaters were there? Like, thirty?"

I put an arm around her. I was just about to say, "It's okay," when Meena hugged me back.

"I skated better than half of these other girls!" she cried, laughing. "Can you believe it?" She looked delighted. More delighted than Jacqui did, honestly. The judges were about to announce the winners, but Jacqui had to know that she was in first place. Still, the tense look on her face told me that she wouldn't believe it until it was official.

Finally, the winners were announced. I skated out and took my place on the podium. A girl in an elaborate yellow lace dress came in second. And Jacqui — of course — took first. One of the girls from the youngest class skated out (a bit wobbly) to place the medal around my neck. I looked down at the bronze. A leaf was stamped on it. CHICAGO NON-QUALIFYING JUNIOR SKATE, it said. It was pretty. I was glad to have it, even if it wasn't a gold medal.

Once the applause was over, I skated back to my friends, who were cheering madly. When we reached the boards, Jacqui took my hand suddenly. "I wanted to tell you — you skated really well." She blushed a little.

"Thanks, Jacqui," I said. "So did you." Then I laughed. "I guess that's pretty obvious." I waved at the gold medal around her neck.

Jacqui sighed and looked down at the medal. "Thanks." She pressed the medal between her hands. "It's heavy," she murmured. She threw back her head and smiled at me. "Mom will be happy."

"Now it's on to the qual?" I asked.

"Yeah. What about you?"

I thought for a moment. "I may just stick with non-qual," I told her.

"You should compete," Jacqui told me. "You're really good. Once you get that axel . . ."

I nodded. "Yeah. Maybe," I told her.

At that moment, our friends clustered around us. "Let me see!" Delia exclaimed. She tugged at my medal, then at Jacqui's. "Honestly, you guys, the silver is the prettiest. It would have looked better with your dress, Rosa."

"You are such a nutburger, Delia," I told her, and she grinned.

"Carleton!" Jacqui cried.

Looking over, I saw Carleton hovering nearby. He was fiddling with the rose in his hand. "Oh, hi," he said, stepping toward us.

I looked over at Meena, who seemed to have shrunk — turtlelike — into the scarf wrapped around her neck.

"That's so sweet of you," Jacqui said, reaching for the rose.

Almost like a reflex, Carleton yanked it back. "Um," he said. His eyes darted over to Meena.

Meena looked down at the rose and let out a gasp. "Is that . . . ?"

"It's a sterling rose," Carleton said.

"Like Olivier gave Martina in Volume Six?" Meena cried.

Carleton blushed even deeper and handed the rose to Meena. "I knew you'd understand," he said.

Atlanta looked at me for a translation. "It's a Grey Shadows thing," I guessed.

Jacqui looked like she was about to fall on the floor, but she recovered. "Oh, that's so sweet of you, to bring that for Meena," she said.

Meena gazed at Carleton, her eyes gleaming like stars.

"I was really bummed you couldn't come bowling the other night," Carleton said. "We . . . I missed you."

"You did?" Meena breathed.

"I'm glad you're feeling better."

"What?" Meena looked blank. "Oh! Right." She grinned. "I'm feeling better. *Way* better!" Meena turned her grin on me, and I couldn't help smiling back.

"Oh, sweetie pie!" I remembered Jacqui's mother from the Athena salon. She made her way over and scooped Jacqui into her arms. "This is wonderful! Wonderful!" She touched Jacqui's medal reverently, and her eyes glistened.

"Thanks, Mom," Jacqui said warmly.

Anton was right behind them, looking like a male model, as usual. He looked at me and gave a sympathetic wince. "You came really close," he said, putting a hand on my arm.

Oh, *ugh. You came really close.* In Spanish, when something sets you off, you say, "*Me cae mal,*" which means "it falls badly with me." That fell very badly with me — like something oozy.

"Yeah, well — I had fun," I said.

"Mmm." Anton looked like he didn't believe me.

That was when I realized something — *Anton and Jacqui don't get along because they're exactly alike. For both of them, you either win, or you're a loser.*

"You stomped!!" someone shouted. When I looked over, I saw Reggie grinning at me. He pulled me into a hug. This time, I wasn't surprised — I hugged back. "You were amazing!"

"Thanks!" I said warmly.

"Except for the part where she fell down," Anton put in.

Reggie gave Anton a confused look. "Dude, are you serious?" he asked. "That was the *best* part — that's when she got back up again!"

Anton cocked his head, as if to say, "Are *you* serious?" But it was obvious Reggie was. That was what was so awesome about him.

He smiled at me, and I noticed how cute it was that his eyes crinkled at the corners. Suddenly, my heart started to flutter again.

How come I never noticed that Reggie is so cute?

Just then, Papi, Mom, and Amelia made their way over.

"You won! You won!" Amelia shouted, nearly squishing me with a hug.

"Well — I came in third," I corrected her.

"You got a medal," Amelia said. "That's incredible!"

My grandfather's eyes were nearly brimming with tears. "*Amorcita*, your grandmother would be so proud," he said.

Mom looked up at Papi. "Oh, Dad," she said, giving him a warm hug. Then she turned to me.

"Sweetheart, that was great. Would you like to have your friends over for some cocoa and buñuelos?"

I looked over at Reggie, who gave me a thumbs-up. "I'm always ready for cocoa," he said. "And I don't know what a bunny-thingie is, but I'll give it a try."

I felt my heart nearly bursting again. "Great," I said. I looked over at Meena, who was still chatting away with Carleton. She kept brushing the lavender rose against her nose, inhaling its scent. I was sure they would come over, too. "Thanks, Mom."

"So, Rosa." Reggie jammed his fists into his pockets. "Just wanted to let you know that I've been working on our report on minerals. It's almost finished. I'll e-mail it to you so that you can edit it before we hand it in to Ms. Fontayne."

"Terrific!" I said. "I finally finished all of my makeup homework, so I can hand in everything tomorrow."

Reggie held up his hand for a high five. "Congrats."

I giggled as I slapped his palm, then had to keep myself from clapping a hand over my mouth. *Wow — a silly giggle for Reggie?*

He gave me a shy smile that made my heart do a little flip.

Just then, Amelia tugged at my elbow, and I leaned close so she could whisper to me. "Laura said you were the best one, and I thought so, too."

I smiled. "I like your new friend already."

"It's too bad Jessica couldn't be here to see you skate," Amelia said.

Reggie had gone over to talk to Meena. She looked up at me and waved. I waved back.

"It's okay," I told Amelia, and I really meant it. It was hard to say good-bye to Jessica, but I had new friends. *Real* friends.

And that was all that really mattered.

TURN THE PAGE FOR THESE
CANDY APPLE SWEET TREATS!

Hair Flair:
The Best Hairstyle for You

Have you ever wanted to find your best hair look? Get a customized Athena Spa hair consultation and add some flair to your hair!

Tired of the same hairstyle but not sure what new cut will be fabulous and flattering? Dreading the possibility of a crazy stylist hacking off your lovely locks? Use this hairstyle helper to determine your unique face shape, as well as the haircut that best complements it.

First, figure out whether you have an oval, oblong, round, square, or heart-shaped face.

Materials:

Hair tie

Mirror

Instructions:

1. Tie your hair back at the base of your neck, so that your ears and neck are exposed. Stand about one foot away from the mirror so that your reflection is clear and true-to-life.

- If the length of your face is approximately one and a half times the width, you have an oval face.
- If the length and width of your face are approximately equal, you have a round face.
- If the length of your face is greater than the width, and the width is the same at the tip of your chin and the top of your forehead, you have an oblong or square face.
- If the width of your face is greatest at the forehead or cheekbones and narrowest at the tip of the chin, you have a heart-shaped face.

2. Now that you have determined your face shape, follow the guidelines below to find your best cut.

- If you have an oval face, you can pull off nearly any style, short or long. Chin-length bobs and wavy, layered styles are particularly flattering, but avoid heavy bangs and hair that covers your perfectly-proportioned face. Also, short layers may add height to the top of your head, making your face appear longer than it is.

- If you have a round face, create the illusion of length with volume and height at the top of your head. Minimize volume around your face with razor-cut ends. Wispy locks and side parts also help to lengthen your face, but stay away from super-short cuts, chin-length hair, or centered parts.

- If you have an oblong or square face, balance the length with side-swept bangs or short to medium styles. Side parts, curls, and outward flips create the look of width, while layers and delicate bangs soften square faces. Steer clear of blunt cuts that pass your shoulders. Or, if you want to experiment with a longer style, get layers at the eye and cheekbone level.

- If you have a heart-shaped face, highlight your high cheekbones with long, side-swept bangs. Styles that are fuller at the ends create the illusion of a wider chin and jawbone and create volume at the back of the head. Short cuts with long top layers and angled bobs, which get longer gradually toward the front, are particularly flattering.

Going to the salon should be relaxing and fun. So if you are still unsure about your best haircut, don't worry! Just bring some magazine clippings of your favorite stars' haircuts and ask your stylist if their 'dos are right for you.

Say It in Spanish

Here are some words and phrases Rosa and her family use in this book, plus a few more handy sayings.

Adiós: Good-bye
Buenos días: Good morning
Buenos noches: Good night
Buñuelos: Dessert made from deep-fried dough,
     often sprinkled with sugar, anise, and cinnamon
¿Cómo estás?: How are you?
     Muy bien, gracias: Very well, thank you
¿Cómo te llamas?: What's your name?
     Me llamo ___: I'm called ___
Empanadas: Pastry shell turnovers filled with
     savory meat or fruit, served deep-fried or baked
Está chévere: That's cool
Gracias: Thank you

De nada: You're welcome

Hola: Hello, hi

Poblanos: Mild, dark green chili peppers that can be prepared dried, roasted, fried, or stuffed

Por favor: Please

¡Que linda!: How pretty!

¿Qué tal?: What's up? How's it going?

¡Qué suerte!: How lucky!

¡Qué horror!: How awful!

Ropa: Clothes

pronunciation Key:

The "ll" sound is pronounced as a "y," like in "yo."

The "ñ" sound is pronounced as an "n" with a "yay" added onto it.

The accent mark indicates a stress over the syllable.

Glam It Up With Glitter

Bring the glimmer of the ice to an everyday outfit with this quick and easy do-it-yourself project!

You can channel the grace and pizzazz of your favorite figure skaters by attaching rhinestones to your clothes or shoes. Not only do rhinestones add some sparkle, they're also a great way to embellish and transform clothes that you already have.

Materials:

A plain T-shirt, pair of jeans, flip-flops, or canvas
    shoes

Rhinestones

Fabric glue (skip this if you're using self-adhesive
    or studded rhinestones)

Toothpick

Flat surface

Piece of newspaper to protect your work surface

Optional: stencil and fabric chalk

Note: You can find rhinestones at your local craft store. They come in a few varieties: plain (to be attached with glue), self-adhesive (often with a peel-off backing so you can easily stick them to most surfaces), and studded (with metal fasteners that poke through fabric and are closed with pliers or a similar tool). The directions below are for plain rhinestones.

Instructions:

1. Prepare your work surface by covering it with newspaper to prevent adhesive spills.
2. Plan your design using a stencil and chalk. Using the chalk to mark the location of each stone, make dots small enough that the rhinestones will cover them completely. Consider adding rhinestones to jeans pockets, along the cuffs, or down the legs. Dress up a plain T-shirt with a sparkling pattern along the neckline or at the hem. Or bedeck a pair of shoes with a pattern along the top opening or at the toe. Your imagination is the limit!

3. Next, test the adhesive on a spare swatch of fabric to ensure that it doesn't damage the material. Then, use a toothpick to cover the back of the first stone with adhesive, and apply it to the marked spot on the fabric.

4. Apply the rest of the rhinestones to complete your design. Be sure to let the adhesive dry for at least 24 hours, or as long as specified on the container.

Cooking with Candy Apple

Try these fun recipes from Rosa's family! And remember to follow these important rules when you're in the kitchen:

- Always ask a parent if it's OK to use the oven or stove.
- Wash your hands before you start cooking.
- Don't forget to clean up the kitchen when you're done cooking!

Homemade Hot Chocolate
(Serves 4)

Ingredients:
4 cups whole milk
½ cup semisweet chocolate chips
2 tablespoons granulated (white) sugar

1 teaspoon ground cinnamon

½ teaspoon vanilla extract

1 pinch of salt

Instructions:

1. Place the chocolate chips, sugar, cinnamon, vanilla, and salt in a small pot or saucepan on low heat, stirring vigorously with a whisk as the chocolate starts to melt. Keep stirring so that chocolate doesn't stick to the bottom of the pot.

2. Add the milk and raise the heat to medium, stirring constantly until the chocolate is dissolved and the milk starts to simmer.

3. Heat for approximately two minutes, stirring constantly so that the mixture doesn't stick to the bottom of the pot or boil.

4. Pour the hot chocolate into four mugs and serve. You can also add a dollop of whipped cream or top with marshmallows.

Mom's Beef Empanadas

(Makes 12)

Ingredients:

For the meat filling:

1 pound ground beef

2 small potatoes, boiled until soft, then peeled and diced into small cubes

1 small onion, peeled and coarsely chopped

3 cloves of garlic, peeled and finely chopped

1 teaspoon ground cumin

½ teaspoon salt

½ teaspoon oregano

¼ teaspoon ground black pepper

1 teaspoon oil

Optional:

¼ cup of green olives, finely chopped

1 hardboiled egg, coarsely chopped

¼ cup raisins, soaked in warm water for an hour

For the dough:

1 box of two premade and rolled pie crusts (typically available in the refrigerated section of your grocery store)

Instructions:

1. Remove the two pie crusts from the packaging, allowing them to come to room temperature.

2. Sauté the onions and garlic in the oil over medium heat for one minute. Add the ground beef, and allow it to brown, mixing with a nonstick spatula. Add the potato and other ingredients. Bring to a simmer and heat until the meat is cooked thoroughly and all ingredients are fully mixed together. Set the filling aside to cool.

3. Preheat the oven to 350°F.

4. Unroll each pie crust, remove the plastic wrap, and divide each crust into approximately six equal portions. This can be done by cutting each crust in half and then cutting each half into three equally-sliced pieces.

5. Mold each piece of dough into a ball using your hands.

6. Lightly flour a flat surface, and roll each piece of dough into a circle, about 4 to 4½ inches in diameter and ¼-inch thick.

7. Place 1½ to 2 tablespoons of filling in the center of each dough circle. The filling should be approximately at room temperature and strained of excess liquid before being placed in the dough.

8. Fold the dough over to make a filled half circle, and use a fork to press the joined edge and crimp it.

9. Place empanadas on a lightly greased baking sheet.

10. Bake for 15 to 20 minutes or until golden brown. Allow the pan to cool on a rack.

A Chat With Lisa Papademetriou

Q: What inspired you to become a writer?

A: I've always loved reading. When I was in middle school, I read a lot of funny books, like Paula Danziger's *The Cat Ate My Gymsuit*. I knew that I wanted to write books like that when I grew up.

Q: What advice do you have for aspiring writers?

A: My advice is to keep writing! I wasn't one of those kids who won a lot of writing awards when I was in school. I just kept working at it because I enjoyed it. It was only later that I realized that other people thought I was funny and liked hearing my stories.

Q: Where do you get your ideas?

A: When something funny happens to me, I often find myself telling everyone I know about it. If enough people laugh, I begin to wonder — is this something that could go in a book? And it usually is!

Q: Do your experiences in middle school inform your characters'?

A: Yes! For example, in *Accidentally Fabulous*, there is a scene in which the main character, Amy Flowers, goes to school dressed as an amoeba for National Science Day. Well, I went to school dressed as fungus for National Science Day — I wore a flowered sheet and sprayed my hair green. Also, in *Accidentally Friends*, there's a scene where Amy squirts Preston Harringford in the face with a squirt gun as she rides past him on a Ferris wheel. Then, when the wheel comes around, he dumps a bucket of water on her! True story for me — only it wasn't a Ferris wheel. It was the Lobster, which has arms that spiral out and whip you around.

Q: When you are not writing, what do you like to do?

A: My main hobby is chasing after my three-year-old daughter, Zara! I also play the guitar, knit, teach writing, and volunteer. And I read, of course!

Check out

Miss Popularity
and the Best Friend Disaster

by Francesco Sedita

Another candy apple book...
just for you.

Erin and Laura looked up from their menus, shocked. "Excuse me?" Erin asked.

Etoile's face was red now and her eyes were wide. "Ever since I've said hello to you two, all you've done is make me feel like an outsider."

Cassie gasped, and glanced at Erin and Laura to see if they would apologize.

No such luck.

"Because you are," Erin said, with a self-satisfied tone. "I'm sorry, Etoile, but you're *not* one of us."

Cassie felt like she was sinking in quicksand. She couldn't figure out how to get them out of this. "Guys, come on," she said gently. "We're in Friendly's! Get it? *Friendly's*?"

But her friends ignored her.

"I am not an outsider!" Etoile snapped back, her face growing redder by the second. "You are in our state now. You are visiting *us*!" Her voice cracked on the last word, and her eyes filled with tears. Cassie felt a pang at the sight.

"We aren't visiting you, we're visiting Cassie. You're just along for the ride," Laura retorted, glaring at Etoile.

"Erin! Laura! Stop!" Cassie said, so upset she thought *she* might cry.

Big tears fell from Etoile's eyes, and she didn't bother to wipe them away. "Oh, please, Cassie," she managed to say through her tears. "Don't bother defending me. It's true. I thought we knew so much about each other and it's clear that we don't."

"We do. And the stuff we don't know, we're learning. That's what friends do!" Cassie said pleadingly, hoping this would all just go away.

"But what about Jonah?" Etoile demanded. "That's a big deal! When were you going to tell me?" she asked, holding back a sob. She put her hand over her mouth.

Cassie sat quietly. She didn't know how to answer.

"*We've* known for a long time," Laura said. She and Erin didn't even look sorry that Etoile was crying.

Cassie put her head in her hands in frustration. "Enough!" she cried.

"You know, I just don't understand," Erin said, her face twisted in annoyance. "We've been in Cassie's life a lot longer than you, and for some reason, you just don't get that or something." Her words were sharp.

Just then, the waitress came over with a big ice-cream sundae, topped with whipped cream and a candle. Erin must have told her to bring it over when she went to the ladies'. Normally, Cassie would have been delighted by her friends being so thoughtful, but instead she just wanted to burst into tears.

The waitress began singing "Happy Birthday" and when no one joined her, she stopped, looked around uncomfortably at the girls, and put the sundae on the table. "Happy birthday, dear," she said and walked away.

Cassie sat there, the candle burning lower and lower. She looked at her unhappy friends. Etoile was wiping her eyes with a napkin, attempting to pull herself together. Erin and Laura were sitting with their arms crossed over their chests, their jaws set. Cassie sighed and made the only wish she could.

I wish they would stop fighting. I wish Maine and Texas would be friends.

She smiled at the girls. "Thanks for the sundae, guys," she said quietly, trying her hardest to be sincere.

She closed her eyes.

She chanted in her head: *Just get along. Get along. Understand that each one of you is the best person on the planet.*

She blew the candle out and the girls clapped weakly.

Would her wish come true?

Accidentally
Fabulous

Accidentally
Famous

Accidentally
Fooled

Accidentally
Friends

How to Be a Girly Girl in
Just Ten Days

Miss Popularity

Miss Popularity
Goes Camping

Making Waves

Juicy Gossip

Life, Starring Me!

Callie for President

Totally Crushed

Wish You Were Here,
Liza

See You Soon,
Samantha

Miss You, Mina

Winner Takes All

POISON APPLE BOOKS

The Dead End

This Totally Bites!

Miss Fortune

Now You See Me...

THRILLING. BONE-CHILLING.
THESE BOOKS HAVE BITE!